So Willing

LAWRENCE BLOCK
DONALD E. WESTLAKE
writing as Sheldon Lord and Alan Marshall

SO WILLING

LAWRENCE BLOCK & DONALD E. WESTLAKE
writing as Sheldon Lord and Alan Marshall

Copyright © 2010 Lawrence Block and
the estate of Donald E. Westlake

All Rights Reserved.

This is a work of fiction. Names, characters, places, and incidents are the products of the author's imagination or are used fictitiously. Any resemblance to actual events, locales, or persons is entirely coincidental.

Cover and Interior Design by QA Productions

A LAWRENCE BLOCK PRODUCTION

Classic Erotica

---

21 Gay Street
Candy
Gigolo Johnny Wells
April North
Carla
A Strange Kind of Love
Campus Tramp
Community of Women
Born to be Bad
College for Sinners
Of Shame and Joy
A Woman Must Love
The Adulterers
Kept
The Twisted Ones
High School Sex Club
I Sell Love
69 Barrow Street
Four Lives at the Crossroads
Circle of Sinners
A Girl Called Honey
Sin Hellcat
So Willing

Classic Erotica #23

SO WILLING

Lawrence Block
Donald E. Westlake

Chapter 1

Vince parked his father's car in front of Betty's house, checked in the glove compartment to be sure he hadn't forgotten the "necessary equipment," smoothed his hair on the left side, where the wind coming in the window had mussed it, and stepped out of the car.

Betty's father was sitting on the porch in his undershirt. It was seven-thirty of an evening late in June, and just twilight. Betty's father was an indistinct figure seen from the street, an expanse of white undershirt and a glowing cigarette, that was all.

Vince frowned. Betty'd told him her parents were going to be out tonight, and he'd planned to bring her back here after the movies. A bed had it all over a backseat any day, particularly with a virgin. Well, the hell with it. The backseat would have to do.

Erasing the frown and replacing it with an easy, deferential smile, Vince walked around the car, across the sidewalk and up the walk. "Hi, Mister Baxter," he said, as he went up the stoop.

"Good evening, Vince."

"Betty ready yet?"

"I don't suppose so. You know how women are."

Mister Baxter chuckled. He had an asinine habit of trying to get on a pals relationship with Betty's dates. It made Vince uncomfortable, but he managed not to show it. If you wanted to get anywhere with a girl you had to get along with her parents. That was rule number one.

Mister Baxter motioned at the screen door. "You might just go on in and see," he said.

"Thanks, Mister Baxter," Vince said. It hadn't taken long with the Baxters, not long at all. He'd taken Betty out three times, and already he was at the stage with her parents where he could just walk into the house. The fact that Mister Baxter worked so damn hard to make everybody like him had helped, of course. Mister Baxter was a sales manager for Modnoc Products, the local plastic company. He'd started as a commission salesman and learned to treat everybody like a long-lost buddy. He still had the habit, combined with an obsession to get along with the younger generation just to prove he wasn't old yet. So Vince hadn't had to work hard to make Mister Baxter like him at all. He'd just shown up that first evening, three weeks ago, smiling politely, a conservatively dressed, good-looking young man of seventeen, and Mister Baxter had fallen all over himself to be chums.

As for Mrs. Baxter, it didn't matter a bit what she thought. Mrs. Baxter was the closest thing to being invisible of anyone Vince had ever met. Not physically invisible—she was about five foot four and weighed nearly two hundred pounds, topped by stringy tight-curled, gray hair and a simpering fat face—but her personality was invisible. Her voice was so faint it was almost non-existent, and if she had any opinions or beliefs or thoughts about anything, she kept them to herself. She inevitably stood around in the background somewhere, smiling her please-don't-hurt-me smile and fumbling with her faded apron. Vince had given her about thirty seconds worth of charm the first time he'd come to the house, and had ignored her ever since.

He ignored her now. He opened the screen door and stepped into the foyer of the house. The stairs to the second floor bedrooms were straight ahead, the living room off to the left. Mrs. Baxter was in the living room, watching some stupid television program, and when she heard the screen door close she looked over, smiling as usual, and in her faded voice said, "Good evening, Vince."

"Hi, Mrs. Baxter," Vince said. He returned her smile for a tenth of a second, and then went forward to the foot of the stairs. "Hey, Betty!" he shouted.

"In a minute!" came the answering shout.

"Sure," Vince said, under his breath. Betty, in her own sweet way, was as bad as her parents.

Mrs. Baxter leaned forward in her chair to say, "Why don't you come in and watch television with me while you wait, Vince?"

The prospect sickened. Vince thought it over for a second. If he went back out on the porch, Mister Baxter, who was convinced that everybody in the whole United States of America was as psycho about baseball as he was, would start jabbering about who did what on the ballfield this afternoon, and Vince couldn't have named three major league ballplayers if his life depended on it. He might even have had trouble naming three major league teams. At least there wouldn't be any conversation with invisible Mrs. Baxter.

"Sure," he said politely. "Thanks a lot."

He went into the living room and sat down facing the television set. His eyes were aimed at the set, but he didn't pay any attention to the blue-gray shadows flitting back and forth across the screen. He spent his time thinking about Betty, who was sixteen and good-looking and well-built and a virgin. His first virgin, by God!

Vince had been fifteen when he had first discovered how easy it was for him to get a girl to go the limit with him. He'd made another discovery at the same time. He discovered why it was that people spent so much of their time thinking about sex and talking about sex and planning for sex and having sex and chasing after sex. It was because sex was the greatest thing since rings with secret compartments. Girls, he had discovered, had secret compartments, too, and they contained a map to paradise. It was farewell Captain Marvel, a new marvel has been found.

Sex was great. Sex was great before, when you were leading up to it, working around like the coolest strategist who ever lived, like a band of Indians sneaking up on the fort, ready to crash through the wall the minute they were close enough. And it was great during, which went without saying. And it was great after, when the girl would look at you like you were God and you knew she'd give anything to have you do it to her again. And it was great even later, when you got together with the other guys, and everybody has sex on the mind, trying to figure out how to get some for themselves, and you could tell them you've had it, and this is what it was like.

For some guys it was tough to get some. For Vince it was the easiest thing in the world. You just had to have the right attitude for it, that was all. You had to see it as a kind of war, with the girl and her parents and adults everywhere as the enemy. First, you had to play sheepdog and break the girl loose from the pack, get her off by herself. Then you had to play the strategist, and that was where Vince had a natural talent.

The thing was, every girl had a Dream Man. Usually, he was some movie star, or maybe a combination of movie stars, or singers, or something like that. You found out who the Dream Man was, what his qualities were, what he was like—and the girl never got tired of talking about her Dream Man, once you got her started—and then you simply showed her you had the exact same qualities the Dream Man had, plus one more quality: You were flesh and blood, and available. And she'd be on her back before you could say, "Unzip."

For two years now, Vince had been sharpening his form, going with girl after girl, and he hadn't grown bored with the game yet. Nor did he think he ever would grow bored with it. But tonight was the first time with a virgin. Every other girl he'd ever had had come to him at least second. And a girl who already knew what sex was all about would naturally be more eager than a girl who'd never had any at all.

He'd tried a couple of virgins, two years ago, shortly after losing his own virginity, and had gotten nowhere. So he'd given up virgins as being more trouble than they were worth, and this was the first time he'd purposely gone after a virgin since.

A virgin, by God, a certified virgin. He'd noticed Betty in school, and had talked with a few guys who had taken her out. According to them, it was impossible to get anywhere at all with Betty. You couldn't even cop a feel without her getting all upset and mad.

She was the one. He knew her casually, from school, and two days before he was due to graduate, he asked her for a date. She'd accepted, as he knew she would, and that first date he'd been as sexless as a spayed cat. They'd gone to the movies, and they'd talked, and they'd had hamburgers, and they'd driven around for a while, and then he'd taken her home, being sure to get her home fifteen minutes before the one o'clock deadline her parents had set. Get along with the parents and you'll get the girl.

The second date had run pretty much like the first, except that they'd parked for a while up at High Point, and necked. He'd kissed her, but he'd kept his hands to himself, and he got her home ahead of schedule again, with a chaste goodnight kiss on her front porch.

The third date, they'd necked at the movies, and she'd responded nicely. By now, he knew a lot about Betty's Dream Man. He was polite and gentlemanly, but he was also the outdoorsy type, the kind who goes off to the woods and lives in a tent, hunting and fishing, every once in a while. And he was frank, outspoken, and sincere.

So that's the way Vince played it. He necked with her in the theater, and then they went back to High Point again and necked some more, and he could feel her getting excited, and at just the right moment he'd pulled away from her and said, "I think we ought to go for a walk and cool off, Betty. I'm having trouble keeping my hands to myself." And he'd gotten out of the car before she could answer and walked around to open the door on her side.

Theirs was the only car at High Point that night, and so they had strolled around for a while, hand in hand, looking down at the scattered lights of the town below them. Vince had talked about the cabin his family owned at a lake in the mountains, upstate, and he had played it as outdoorsy as he possibly could. He had also talked about the trouble he was having keeping his hands off her, and he was very honest and sincere—and flattering—about it. By the time they got back into the car, she knew he was her Dream Man, and she knew he wanted her.

He didn't even have to make the first move. When he kissed her, she reached out and took his hand and laid it against her breast, and whispered, "It's all right, Vince, it really is."

Maybe he could have had her that night. He didn't know. He wasn't sure, and he hadn't tried. He had the program set up, and he was following it. That night, he had gotten her blouse open and her bra off. He had touched her breasts—lovely full breasts for a sixteen-year-old, pink-tipped and firm—and kissed them. He had slid his hand up the inside of her leg and touched her with slow, lingering fingers, and she had closed her eyes and sighed, and her hands had been taut on his back.

But he'd stopped. He'd played it sincere and gentlemanly, he'd been the original Square Shooter, and he had shot not. And he even got her home by curfew time. The goodnight kiss on the front porch that night had been combined with two busy hands, and he had left her to go to bed with the hot memory of his left hand on her breast and his right hand up under her skirt.

And tonight was the night the program culminated. Tonight, Vince was going to get himself a certified virgin. Already he had gone farther with her than anyone he knew—and the guys he knew weren't reticent about their conquests or near-conquests—and tonight he would finish the job. He was leaving for the cabin by the lake soon, and this would be just about the last chance.

Betty had told him that her parents were going to be out tonight, and he'd planned on coming back to the house early. He'd checked the TV listings and found out what movie was going to be on the Midnight Show, and he would have told her how much he had been looking forward to seeing this movie. It was some old World War Two movie about counterspies and Gestapo agents and all that jazz, which he wanted to see like he wanted to fall down a manhole, but he didn't plan on watching much of it.

Now, there was Mister Baxter out on the front porch, in his undershirt, and there was Mrs. Baxter, sitting across the living room in her flower-print dress and faded apron, and it seemed pretty clear that neither of them was intending to go anywhere at all. Which meant it was going to have to be the backseat of the car, or maybe on a blanket if he could find someplace secluded enough. And he had been looking forward to making his first virgin in her own bed.

And here came the virgin now, down the stairs, her blonde hair pulled back in a ponytail, her full breasts jutting out against an electric blue sweater, the center of interest wrapped in a hip-tight gray skirt. Vince got up, smiling at her, and she smiled back, saying something about being sorry for her lateness.

The goodbyes were over with quickly. Mrs. Baxter had said, "Have a good time," and Betty had answered, "You have a good time, too," and they had gone out to the porch, where Betty had the exact same exchange with her father, and then they went down to the car, a '57 Dodge, cream and green, with beige fins. Vince, the perfect gentleman, held the right-hand door open while Betty slid into the seat, clutching her skirt down at her knees. He closed the door once she was settled, and went around to his own side. He glanced back at the house just before getting into the car. Mister Baxter was still sitting on the porch in his undershirt, and Mrs. Baxter was standing in the doorway, her nose not quite touching the screen, her round shape framed by the living room lights behind her. Simultaneously, as though some director off in the bushes on the next-door lawn had given them a signal, they both raised their right hands and waved. Vince waved back, and got into the car.

In that quick glance, he had also noticed again the wooden fire-escape on the side of the house. This was a residential district, all two-story one-family houses, but after a trio of bad fires in houses of this type, a town ordinance had been passed making it compulsory to have an outside stairway in any house where people lived on more than one floor. The wooden fire-escape, Vince had learned after gentle questioning, led to Betty's bedroom. Since learning that, he had entertained idle daydreams about crawling up that fire escape and spending a few quiet hours in Betty's bedroom and in Betty's bed. But that was strictly daydreaming. That wasn't the way to get her, sneaking through windows at three o'clock in the morning. The way to get her was to make her want to be gotten.

Vince started the car and drove down to the corner, then turned left toward downtown. "I thought your parents were going out tonight," he said, as casually as he could.

"They are," she answered.

"Wearing undershirt and apron?"

"Oh, they don't have to leave the house till nine o'clock. And it's only a little after seven-thirty now. They've got ages."

"Where they going?"

"A surprise party for my Uncle George up in Votzburg. The party doesn't start till eleven. My Aunt Edna is keeping him out of the house till then."

"Votzburg is forty miles away from here," he said, surprised that Betty's parents would be going, of their own free will, more than ten feet from the house.

"I know," she said disinterestedly. She couldn't care less what her parents did.

Vince calculated rapidly. The party was going to start at eleven o'clock. It would have to run a couple of hours anyway, until around one, maybe two. Betty's old man would have half a bag on by the time he left the party, and the road from Votzburg was narrow, winding, hilly and two lanes wide. Forty miles of that road, at two or three o'clock in the morning, with half a bag on. They wouldn't be home before four a.m. at the earliest.

He smiled. "You know," he said, "I was looking at the paper tonight, at the TV listings." He forced enthusiasm into his voice. "And do you know what's playing—?"

They got back to the house at a quarter to twelve. In the movie, he had spent the first half of the double feature with his arm around Betty's shoulders, occasionally leaning over to kiss her, his free hand clasping hers. The second half, he'd progressed. The arm around her shoulder had drawn in tighter, so the hand dangled down over her breast, just barely brushing the tip of it at first and then gradually touching it more insistently, holding it and stroking it and squeezing it. Their kisses had become longer and fiercer, his tongue searching and probing deeply within her mouth, and her breathing was faster, her eyes bright in the dimness of the movie theater. His other hand had touched her knee, slid under the hem of her skirt, stroked slowly up the inside of her thigh, and she squirmed in the seat, whispering, "Oh. Oh."

In the car, he had driven one-handed. His other arm was around her, the hand reaching around to massage her breast, as he had done in the theater. She sat close to him, her breath hot and fast in his ear, and she had begun to grow bold herself. Her hand had rested on his leg, and he knew that she wanted to touch him as he had touched her. And he also knew she was going to get the opportunity very soon.

They got to the house at a quarter to twelve, and Vince immediately sat down on the sofa, expecting Betty to come sit beside him. But she said something about coffee and went out to the kitchen. He followed her out, saying, "Who wants coffee?"

"I do," she told him.

He stood in the kitchen doorway. "Betty," he said.

She stopped her fussing with cups and saucers. Her back was to him, and slowly she turned to face him. Her eyes were bright, as they had been in the movie, but they showed wariness, too.

"Come into the living room, Betty," he said. "Come sit with me in the living room."

"I was—going to make coffee," she said hesitantly.

"Never mind the coffee. Come on in the living room."

She hesitated a moment longer, and then smiled and said, "All right."

They went back to the living room, and this time she sat down on the sofa beside him, but almost immediately moved to get up again, saying, "You didn't turn the TV set on."

He grabbed her arm, pulling her back down on the sofa. "We've got fifteen minutes yet," he said. "All that's on now is news and weather. Who cares about news and weather?"

She was half-turned, facing him, and she smiled again, her eyes brighter than ever. "Nobody does," she said. And when he reached for her, she came soft and eager into his arms.

But it wasn't as easy as he'd thought. She let him French kiss her, she let him fondle her breasts and slide his hand up the inside of her leg, she let him push the sweater up and open her bra, she let him touch the bare breasts, pinching the hard tips gently between his fingers, kissing her breasts, but when his hand, beneath her skirt, slid up to grab the waist of her panties and slide them down, she pulled away from him at once, pushing the offending hand away, whispering, "No, Vince. We can't go that far. No."

He was obedient, that time. He let his hand slide down again across her silk-covered belly, and pulled her close to kiss her again, to touch her breasts with fingers and lips and tongue.

He waited. Stroking her, kissing her, caressing her, nipping her flesh with his teeth. He waited until her eyes were closed and her mouth was open and her breath was loud and short and ragged, her arms limp and weak around him, her hips writhing and revolving on the sofa. Then he made the move again, and this time she didn't stop him, and her panties slid away to the floor. And when he touched her, she groaned and clutched him tight to her.

He undressed her there in the living room, piece by piece. The sweater went and the bra, and finally the skirt. And when she was nude and pliant in his arms, he whispered, "Let's go upstairs." And she nodded, whispering, "Yes, Vince, yes."

She led the way up the stairs and he followed, pulling off his shirt and undershirt on the way. She walked ahead of him, her firm round buttocks moving as she climbed the stairs, and he stroked their roundness, wanting to bite them.

Up on the second floor, he started into the first bedroom he came to, but she said, "No, that's my sister's room. My room is down here."

"Your sister." He hadn't known there was a sister. He suddenly felt cold. What if the sister were to come in while he was in the bedroom with Betty? There'd be hell to pay.

His thoughts must have shown on his face, for she laughed and said, "Don't worry. She doesn't live here anymore. She got married two years ago and moved to Denver."

"Oh." Weak with relief, he hurried after Betty to her bedroom.

He had his clothes half off, holding them in one hand. When they reached the bedroom he whipped the rest off right away. He knew the danger in letting the emotion of the moment be washed away by too much time spent on the mechanics of the thing, on the moving to the proper room or from the front seat to the backseat of the car, or getting the clothes off. The mechanics had to be gotten over and done with fast, before they could spoil the mood.

Her room was large and airy and girl-styled, but he didn't notice a thing in it except the three-quarter bed. The covers were turned neatly back, the sheets were crisp and clean, and already he could visualize Betty atop the bed and himself atop Betty.

She sat down on the edge of the bed and raised her arms to him, smiling. He came into her arms, sat beside her, kissed her and stroked her, slowly laid her back and down onto the bed.

"I won't hurt you," he whispered, reassuring her. "You don't have to worry, I won't hurt you."

They were lying crosswise on the bed and gradually they shifted position until they were lying the right way, she on her back and he on his side next to her, still stroking her and kissing her and very gradually rolling forward onto her.

"I've never done this before, Vince," she whispered suddenly.

He was terrified that she would suddenly stop him at the last second, that she would realize she was about to become an ex-virgin, and wouldn't go through with it. "I know," he whispered. "But don't worry, Betty, wonderful wonderful Betty, don't worry."

"You've got to promise," she whispered, and her hands were suddenly firm against him, not pushing him away but not letting him get any closer either. "You've got to promise," she repeated, "not to ever tell anybody. Not anybody."

"I never will," he promised fervently. "I'd never do a thing like that."

"This is the first time," she whispered.

"I know."

"My sister," she explained, whispering in his ear, "always told me to never do it with a boy from my own school or my own town, because that way I'd get a bad reputation. She said I should only go for boys from other towns. I've never done it before. You're the first boy from our school I've ever done this with."

The full import didn't hit him for a couple of seconds, and then he practically yelped. She wasn't a virgin! She wasn't a virgin, after all! He almost said it aloud, as an incredulous, shocked, screamed question: "You're not a virgin!?" But he stifled it just in time, because that question would have ruined the whole thing. He would never been able to explain why it was so important to him that she be a virgin without destroying the mood, and without destroying his chances with her forever.

She was still whispering to him, earnestly and matter-of-factly, and he knew at last that this girl was far from being a virgin. "So you've got to promise never to tell anybody. I don't want to get a bad reputation."

He swallowed, forced himself to answer her. "I won't tell, Betty. Believe me, I won't."

She kissed him and smiled. "The first night we went out," she told him, "I knew I had to have you. No matter what my sister said."

And who, he wondered, had been stalking whom? He felt suddenly young and inexperienced.

"Well, come on," she whispered. "What are you waiting for?"

She was no virgin. There wasn't a virgin in the world who could move like that. She was no virgin, and after thirty seconds it no longer mattered a tinker's dam that she wasn't a virgin. Because she was the most tremendous bed-partner he'd ever held in his arms.

She tore him apart. She was a wild thing, grabbing him with a violence he'd never known before, squeezing him dry like a grape and flinging him away again. And it was over before it was barely begun, and he was lying beside her in the narrow bed, panting, the sweat cooling and drying on his belly and chest, as she leaned over him, kissing him, licking his face, stroking his chest.

He regained his wind slowly, and finally started, "You—you—"

Once again, she understood what he was trying to say. "There's nothing to worry about," she told him, smiling. "I checked on the calendar this afternoon. This is the safe time."

There were voices downstairs!

"It's my parents!" Her whisper in his ear was terrified.

He crawled off the bed and to his feet. He took one step toward the door, but he could hear them coming upstairs.

"They'll look in here," she was whispering. "They always look in to see if I'm asleep."

His wildly searching eye fell on the luminous dial of her bedside clock. It was almost four-thirty in the morning. He should have been out of here long ago, instead of falling asleep like a dope.

"Down the fire escape," she whispered urgently. "Hurry!"

"My clothes!"

"I'll throw them down to you. Hurry, Vince, hurry!"

He had one leg over the windowsill before he realized he was stark naked. Then he remembered the car, still parked out in front of the house. "The car," he whispered.

He saw the shock on her face, and thought fast. "Tell them," he said, "tell them something went wrong with the starter, and I took a bus home, and I said I'd come back in the morning and fix it."

She nodded. "All right. Now, hurry." And she ran around the room, gathering up his clothes.

He went out the fire escape and down the wooden steps, rough against his bare feet. At the bottom step, he carefully lowered himself, until he was hanging by his outstretched hands, facing the street.

Clip-clop. A horse went by, pulling a milk wagon. The milkman stared at Vince, swinging back and forth, his toes three feet from the ground, completely nude. Vince stared at the milkman, and the horse calmly clip-clopped by, and Vince's clothes went sailing down past his face.

He dropped to the ground, fumbled around until he had his clothes in a jumbled bundle in his arms, and ran for the backyard.

There was a shade tree in the backyard. Hidden by it, he hurriedly dressed, then climbed over the fence to the yard of the house on the next street, out to the street, and headed for the nearest bus stop.

"A week from now," he grumbled to himself, as he walked along with his shoelaces flapping, "I'll think this was funny as hell."

Chapter 2

Everything, as a matter of fact, stank. Everything stank out loud, and in spades. And with everything stinking so thoroughly it was no wonder that he wasn't laughing himself silly.

In a sense, you could blame everything on Betty. There she was, all pure virginal, and there he was, all ready and willing, the experienced hunter tracking down the soft-eyed doe, when all of a sudden his whole frame of reference was shattered. Betty the virgin had suddenly metamorphosed into Betty the old hand.

That got things going to a fine start.

When the family left two days later for the cabin on the lake he was not at all sorry to say a fond goodbye to the little town of Modnoc. He'd sprawled alone in the backseat of the car while his mother and father said stupid things to each other in the front seat, and he'd looked back at the town out of the rear window, thinking unpleasant thoughts about it.

As the sun goes out to sea, he thought, *and as our boat sinks slowly in the west, we bid a fond adieu to the sleepy town of Modnoc, with its friendly huts and its rudely plastered natives.*

The cruddy little cabin by the cruddy little lake looked a good deal better to him than it really was. The idea of staying in the same town with Betty made him feel little weak in the knees. Of course there was no reason for him to be ashamed of himself. As far as she was concerned, he was the conqueror, the only boy from Modnoc who had managed to get in her pants. From his point of view it was a little more complex. He'd been loaded for bear, and when you're loaded for bear you can't get too excited over blowing the tail off a squirrel.

So the cruddy little cabin by the cruddy little lake represented two things—an escape from Betty and a chance at new fields to conquer. There would certainly be girls at the lake, plenty of them, and girls away for the summer were girls removed from the soppy security of the parental abode. If a girl was ever going to take the plunge, she was going to take it on summer vacation.

And if anybody was ready to do the plunging for them, Vince was.

He felt like the Great White Hunter, and he was so pleased with the picture that the discomforts of the safari failed to bother him. He didn't mind the lousy roads, or the creative stupidity of his father who insisted on driving a steady thirty-five every inch of the way. He didn't mind the stomach-churning food at the hot dog stands where they stopped en route, he didn't mind the senseless patter issuing from the front seat. He was the Great White Hunter on the trail of a pack of virgins. The little hardships of the chase didn't bother him a bit.

When they finally got to the cabin it looked much better to him than it really was. A kitchen, furnished with colonial implements and quietly disintegrating. A bedroom for his parents. Another bedroom, incredibly small, for Vince. A living room that no one in his right mind would attempt to live in. The cabin was looking around for a president to be born in it, and anyone born there could certainly boast of humble origins.

But Vince didn't care. He didn't figure he'd be spending much time there. He'd be with girls, around girls, near girls, by the side of girls.

And, eventually, in girls.

But things weren't working according to plan. Right now, for example, the afternoon was in the process of becoming evening. It was cool, with a breeze coming from the lake that was just a little too brisk to be perfect. The sun was gone and the moon was starting to rise. It was perfect weather for girl-hunting, and what was he doing?

He was sitting. Sitting quite alone by the side of the lake with nothing doing, nothing at all.

All because of that bitch, Rhonda.

The trouble with Rhonda was double trouble. She was impossible to touch and impossible to stay away from. The first day he saw her, which was the second day at the cabin, he knew she was going to be the one. She just had to be. She was perfect.

For one thing, she was different from any of the Modnoc girls. She was from New York City, and this made a big difference. Not just the way she talked, but the way she looked and the way she acted. She was far more mature, far more sophisticated.

And far more attractive.

Of course, if Vince himself had come from New York, he would have thought that Rhonda looked exactly like everyone else. She had dark hair and she wore it long, and the ponytail that hung to her waist looked just like the ponytail of every other girl who went to Bronx Science or Walden or Elizabeth Irwin or

Music & Art or New Lincoln High School. She also wore sandals and dark-colored Bermuda shorts and very plain white blouses. She was in uniform, but of course Vince did not know this.

Vince thought she was beautiful. The purple eye-shadow was beautiful, too, and the pale lipstick. But most of all, the girl underneath all the garbage was beautiful.

And obviously a virgin.

She was the only one he wanted. There were other girls at the lake, but next to Rhonda they seemed pretty pallid and dull. They could have been easy, some of them. A few gave him come-on glances that meant he could have them flat on their pretty backsides just by saying the word. But he didn't feel like saying the word, not to them.

But Rhonda, damn her to hell, didn't want to hear the word.

All she wanted to do was talk, and walk around in the woods, and go out rowing on the lake, and look at the stars, and think very deep thoughts. This fooled him at first. He dated her about five minutes after he first set eyes on her, and when he asked her what she wanted to do that night she told him she wanted to go rowing on the lake.

Which pleased Vince no end.

Because, as everybody knew, a girl who wants to go rowing on the lake is a girl who wants to do other things. And if the girl herself suggests the rowing expedition it is an odds-on bet that the rowboat is going to get one hell of a workout.

That wasn't exactly the way it turned out. When Rhonda said she wanted to go rowing on the lake, that was precisely what she meant. She wanted to sit in her end of the boat and look up at the stars and think profound thoughts. That was all she wanted to do.

Fortunately, he figured this out before he made the mistake of making a pass. Otherwise everything would have been shot to hell right at the start. But he played things very cool, very cool indeed, staying on his side of the boat and helping her stare at the stars. In between staring at the stars and leaning on the oars he did some supplementary staring at Rhonda's breasts. The blouse she wore was trying to hide the fact that she had any breasts, but Vince had a good eye for that sort of thing. He could tell that she was built very well, soft and firm and very nice to look at, and undoubtedly still nicer to hold onto.

She was, he decided, worth waiting for. So what if she wasn't going to fall into his arms on the first date? Maybe things worked differently in New York.

And, following this line of reasoning, he didn't try to kiss her goodnight. He just stopped her at the door to her cabin, took her chin in his hand, and looked deeply into her eyes. Her eyes were brown and very soft.

"Tomorrow night," he said. She hesitated, then nodded, and he turned on his heel and walked off into the night. He had it made, he knew, because he had suddenly figured out Rhonda's Dream Man. Her Dream Man was sort of a cross between Tony Perkins and Cary Grant, if such a combination was possible. Shy and deep like Perkins, polished and assured like Grant. All he had to do was play that role properly and the prize was his.

Maybe.

The next night was a disappointment. They took a walk to the woods, another type of scene which with any other girl would have been an obvious prelude to a more advanced form of entertainment. Not with Rhonda, however. They walked through the woods and she rambled on and on about how wonderful nature was while he half-listened and half-contemplated how wonderful nature really was.

When he tried to kiss her goodnight she pulled away from him, her eyes very sad. "Don't, Vince." He didn't say anything.

"I like you, Vince. But it's so... so physical, kissing and all that. I'd like us just to be friends, to share things with each other."

He felt like telling her something she had that she really ought to share with him. But that of course would have ruined it for good, so he played his role and hung his head and told her that he was sorry, that of course she was right, and that it was his fault that he had permitted himself to get carried away by animalistic desires.

When he got home he took a cold hip bath, as recommended in that corny Boy Scout Manual. It didn't help.

And if that was bad, the next few nights were worse. Bit by bit he managed to convince her that an experience couldn't be meaningful unless bodies as well as souls merged. While he told her this he kept his hands to himself, speaking slowly and soulfully. And she agreed, more or less.

More or less. Oh, she wasn't one to minimize the importance of physical love. She knew how wonderful a thing physical love could be, when two people shared everything there was to share. There was just one little catch. She herself, she explained sadly, was a cold woman. She couldn't feel anything that way, couldn't get excited or interested. It just didn't do anything for her.

"I'll help you, Rhonda," he told her. "Let me kiss you. Let me make you feel our love."

She was willing to be kissed. So he kissed her, first gently and then not so gently. But kissing her wasn't nearly as pleasant as it should have been. She didn't struggle or pull away. She didn't respond, either. She just stood there like a window dummy and let him do the kissing.

It was about as stimulating as kissing a dead fish.

He kept trying. When the kisses didn't do anything he tried touching her and, although his hands had been itching to get hold of her body, the act itself didn't live up to his expectations.

The body did. He didn't undress her, just ran his hands over her clothing. It was enough to convince him that all that was there belonged to little Rhonda. And little Rhonda was not little at all. She had as nice a body as anyone he had ever came across.

Her breasts were better than Betty's—a little larger and quite a bit firmer. Her legs were perfect.

But all she did was submit to his touches. She didn't quiver or breathe hard or clutch at him or anything. She just acquiesced, and her body as a result was not the body of a warm girl but the body of a very well-formed statue. Perfect and flawless, but no more responsive than a slab of marble.

And somehow this took all the fun out of it. At first it was a challenge, trying to find some way to coax a response out of her. Then, as he kept meeting the challenge and failing wretchedly, it began to become a bit of a bore. Especially because of the way she talked.

They would kiss (or rather he would kiss her) and they would pet (or rather he would pet her) and every few minutes she would pull her head to one side and start telling him how miserable she felt over the fact that she didn't feel a thing. It was bad enough knowing that she didn't feel a thing without hearing about it all the goddamned time. That made things just so much worse.

It was a week now, a week of frustration that didn't seem to be getting him anywhere in particular. And the fact that there was so much other stuff available didn't help matters. He would see girls down by the lake and know damned well that they'd spread their pretty selves for him the minute he said the word.

And here he was with Rhonda.

Who wouldn't.

He had a date with her in half an hour, but somehow he didn't even feel like going. To hell with her. Let her sit in her cabin and play with herself or something. There wasn't any sense wasting his time with her. And it was sure as hell a waste of time. Maybe some of the guys would be all excited at the prospect of playing doctor with a pretty girl, but he'd been around long enough to want more.

To hell with her. He could go out now and find himself something within five minutes, something that would come across on the first date and be all ready and willing any time he wanted. That made one hell of a lot more sense than wasting his time on a hunk of ice from the big bad city of New York.

He hung his head in disgust. The Great White Hunter was out of his class, that was the trouble. He just wasn't good enough to drag down this particular prey.

And then, suddenly, he stopped hanging his head and began to shake it resolutely. Dammit, he wasn't giving up! And he wasn't going to play games any more, either. He was going to win.

He got up, went back to the cabin, got the keys to the car from his father and drove into town. The man at the liquor store was decent enough not to ask to see his draft card. He bought a gallon jug of red wine, knowing that wine was the only drink that had a chance of working on her. Beer was too vulgar and liquor was too strong. Wine would appeal to the romantic side of her, and that was what he wanted.

It didn't seem fair, somehow. But it was no time to worry about fairness. He was going to use the wine, and the wine was going to get her drunk as a skunk, and then he was going to have Rhonda and get her out of his system so that he could concentrate on other girls. This virgin bit was a pain in the neck. Maybe once he got his first virgin out of the way he'd be able to concentrate on bigger and better things.

Although, when you stopped to think about it, it wasn't easy to imagine any bigger and better things than the two big and good things under her blouse.

He hopped back in the car, put the jug of red wine in the backseat and broke some speeding laws on the way to her cabin, which was no mean trick in his father's car. She was waiting for him, and, happily, her parents weren't around. Coming on strong for the parents was a big thing with him, and it was sort of annoying that it was so useless with Rhonda's parents. They didn't really care who she went out with and she didn't care what her parents thought about him, so talking to them was a total waste of time.

"Come with me," he told her mysteriously. "Tonight is our night."

He led her to the car and drove off to the lake. "We're having a picnic," he explained. "A special place that I've never taken you to before. It's sort of a private place of mine."

The place, he went on to explain, was an island in the middle of the lake. What he didn't bother explaining was that he usually avoided the island because it was the dullest spot in the world.

He led her to the rowboat, carrying the jug of wine in one hand. She asked him what the wine was for and he told her a picnic was just not a picnic without a jug of wine. She seemed to accept the explanation.

Rowing across the lake was a real pain in the neck, but he was so fired up at the prospect of finally getting at Rhonda that the rowing didn't bother him as much as it usually did. It was, he reflected, a nice night for seducing a virgin. Dark, quiet, just a moon in the sky with no stars out.

"The wine will be good," he explained. "You see, there's been something wrong with our relationship."

Relationship was one of her favorite words.

"I know," she said. "I know, Vince."

"The wine will help," he told her. "It will relax you, which is the important thing. You'll be able to escape from your inhibitions."

Inhibitions was another of her favorite words.

"I suppose so," she said.

"And after all," he went on, determined to fit her two favorite words into the same sentence, "inhibitions can damage a relationship."

"You're right, Vince," she said. "You're right."

They beached the boat and climbed out onto the crummy little island. Instantly she started going into orbit over what a beautiful private place it was and how glad she was that he liked her enough to share it with her. While she talked on and on he managed to pull the cork out of the wine jug with his teeth.

"Come with me," he said. "Sit by my side."

She sat with him.

"Here," he said. "Drink some of the wine."

She took the jug and tilted it, taking a healthy swallow. He waited for her to choke on it but she didn't. Instead she passed him the jug, her eyes shining.

"It's good wine, Vince."

He tried a sip and decided that either she was off her nut or that he just plain didn't like wine. But it didn't much matter. The important thing was getting the wine into her. He didn't have to drink anything himself.

So he passed the jug back to her.

She took another swig and this time her eyes were very dreamy. When she spoke, her voice was husky.

"I think you're right, Vince. I think maybe the wine is a good idea. It might relax me. It might push my inhibitions to one side so that the real person can shine through."

"Sure," he said.

"I want the real person to shine through, Vince. I don't want to be inhibited forever. You know that, don't you, Vince?"

"Sure," he said. He handed the wine back to her and she took another drink. Then she kicked off her sandals and stretched out on the ground.

"Makes me sleepy," she said. "I have to lie down, Vince."

His heart jumped. It was working. Evidently she wasn't used to drinking. Hell, she was young. Maybe this was the first time anybody'd ever given her anything stronger to drink than a glass of chocolate milk. Whatever it was, he knew he'd picked the right way to do it. If it was cheating to get a girl drunk, well, that was just too bad. If it was cheating; he was a cheat. It was working, and that was all he cared about.

"Vince—"

"What is it, Rhonda?"

"Come lie down next to me."

She didn't have to ask him a second time. It was the first time she'd ever wanted him near her—other times she'd merely accepted him. So he stretched out beside her and took her in his arms.

At first he thought it was going to be different. When he kissed her her lips pressed hard against his and her arms went around him, holding him tight. For a second, just a second, he thought the wine had done its work.

Then she relaxed completely. She was a statue again, a hunk of plaster.

He went on kissing her, forcing his tongue between her parted lips, running his hands over her body. But it wasn't doing him a bit of good. He was getting excited, but that wasn't important. The important thing was to get her excited.

"It's no use, Vince."

"Don't worry." Trying desperately to sound tender instead of obeying the impulse and snarling at her. "Everything's going to be all right, Rhonda. There's nothing for you to worry about."

"But it's not fair. I want to like it, Vince. I want to feel it."

"I know you do."

"But I just can't."

"Of course you can," he said automatically. "Of course you can, dear."

"I can't."

He sat up, reaching for the wine, and he told her that of course she could, that for a moment she had started to respond.

"I felt you getting... excited," he said. He had almost said *hot*.

"For a second, but—"

"That's a beginning," he went on. "Have a little more wine. That should do it for you."

She took the wine from him and he sighed with relief when she started to raise it to her lips. Then suddenly, she lowered it. Her eyes were troubled.

"Vince," she said, "what will happen after I drink enough of the wine?"

"I'll kiss you."

"I know that. I mean—we won't go all the way, will we?"

"Of course not."

"That's good," she said. "I... I can't help being worried. I know you wouldn't try to do anything... wrong, but I can't help worrying."

"You don't have to worry with me," he said.

"I know it, Vince."

"I'm not that kind of a person."

"Oh, I know, Vince."

"I wouldn't try to take advantage of somebody like you, Rhonda."

"I know."

"I'm just doing this for you. That's why I bought the wine—so that you'll learn to relax. It hurts me to see you so tense all the time."

He felt like telling her where it hurt.

"I know, Vince."

"And for us," he went on, wondering if Hollywood would give him a job if they heard him. "I'm doing it for us, so that we can be closer together."

"I know, Vince."

"Drink some wine."

She drank some wine.

"Have another drink, Rhonda. I think it'll do you good."

"Do you really think so?"

He nodded, and she had another drink. This time when she put the jug down he could see how flushed her cheeks were.

He knew just how to play it. After each swig of wine he would kiss her and stroke her as long as she went on responding, and the minute she stopped he would stop also. Then he'd get some more wine into her stomach and start in where he left off.

It was time to begin.

He stretched out beside her and reached for her. This time the kiss was good all the way—her mouth was hot and eager and her tongue matched his own tongue in passion. He hadn't been prepared for that strong a response and for a minute he thought somebody had sneaked up and switched girls on him. But no, nobody else had a body like the one pressed up against him.

He worked expertly, kissing her, stroking the nape of her neck with the fingers of one hand and fondling her breast with the other hand. He kept waiting for the wine to wear off and for the responses to cease, but the responses just got stronger.

He began unbuttoning her blouse. Now, he thought, she was going to stop him.

But she didn't.

He unbuttoned all the buttons and managed to lift her up so that he could get the blouse off. While he had her that way, he got up the nerve to unsnap her bra and get that off, and once he got rid of the bra and there was nothing between him and those breasts, it was no longer a question of nerve. There was just no stopping, not for him.

"Don't, Vince. We don't want to lose control. We have to be careful, Vince."

He wanted to pick up a rock and crack her skull with it. Somehow he forced himself to remain patient. "There's nothing to worry about," he told her. "I can control myself, Rhonda. I just want to touch you. You like it when I touch you, don't you?"

Her answer was a kittenish purr.

And then they were both naked and their bodies were touching and she was more excited than any girl he had ever been with in his life. He knew that she was ready, ready for him, and he was certainly ready for her. More than ready. He couldn't wait any longer.

It began, and he was surprised that she didn't feel any pain. There was supposed to be pain with a virgin. That was what everybody said. But everybody was evidently wrong, because Rhonda was taking to it like a duck to water. She was having a ball.

When it was over she started to cry. He calmed her, reassured her, told her everything was all right.

"I didn't want it to happen," she said. "I was afraid it would happen. And it did."

"We couldn't help ourselves," he told her. It was a good line for this sort of situation.

"You liked it," he said. "Didn't you?"

She nodded.

"Well," he said, "that's the important thing. You got rid of your inhibitions."

"Of course," she said. "I always do when I drink." He just looked at her.

"Every single time," she said. "But only when I drink. With Norman and with Phil and with Johnny and with Dave and Allen and Robert. Every time I drink it's all right and I like it, but I like it so much that I can't stop. That's the bad part. I always go all the way when I drink. I just can't help it."

He couldn't believe it. He knew instinctively that it was true, all true, but he just plain didn't want to believe it.

"It's very strange," she said, her voice almost clinical. "I suppose it's a reaction formation. I'm all repressed and inhibited, and then when I lose my inhibitions I lose all control and I just have to go all the way."

She looked sad, then grinned. He had never seen her grin that way.

"But it's worth it," she said. "Pass me the wine, Vince. I'll have a little more wine and then we can do it again."

Chapter 3

Oh well, what the hell, there was always Adele. Once Vince had managed to unload Rhonda, he'd checked the available quail, and decided that Adele was next.

Not that it was all that easy to unload Rhonda. When Rhonda lost her inhibitions, she had a hell of a time finding them again. After that first night, out at the island, she'd been ready for wining and twining on a steady basis, and Vince was to be the lucky guy.

They had a relationship now, that was the thing. That was the way Rhonda saw it, anyway. They had a relationship, and so now her inhibitions and complexes and mental blocks were all soothed and quieted, as far as Vince was concerned. But not as far as any other guy was concerned. Vince was the only one she could feel really free with. That was the way she expressed it. He was the only one she could feel really free with.

And did she want to feel really free! She wanted it as much as she could get it.

So it wasn't too easy to unload Rhonda. Every time he turned around, there she was, the old gleam in her eye and a bottle of wine in her hand. Vince finally had to resort to psychological double-talk himself.

"I think our relationship is strained," he told her. He knew something was strained, or would be if they kept on like this. "It's because," he told her, "you still need the wine. I can't feel as though it's really me you want. Do you understand?"

Of course she did. She understood completely, and it was a very natural reaction. But she also had the solution. They'd go out to the island without any wine, and they'd see what would happen.

"I bet I don't really need any wine," she said, and rubbed against him a little bit.

He was pretty sure she was right. But he hadn't gotten over his disappointment that the little bitch hadn't been a virgin after all. All he wanted between Rhonda and himself anymore was distance. And lots of it.

He told her he thought they ought to part for a while, that it was time to test their relationship and see if it was really strong. And the only way to do that was to not see each other for a while. Then, when they met again, if the relationship, if the feeling between them—"simpatico" she murmured at that point, nodding—if the feeling between them was still strong, they'd know they really had a solid and lasting relationship on their hands.

She agreed, finally, though with reluctance. And off she went, preceded by her chest, and Vince mopped his brow and went swimming.

Then he lolled around for a couple of days, trying to talk himself into calling off the virgin-hunt.

He gave himself lots of good reasons. He lay around out on the strip of sand between the cabin and the water, soaking up sun and counting off the reasons on his fingers.

The reasons: In the first place, it was by now obvious to him that you could never tell for sure whether a girl was a virgin or not. Her own statements on the subject were worse than useless, of course, and even her actions didn't mean much. Nor did her reputation. Nor did her appearance.

In the second place, virgin-hunting was one of the most frustrating and annoying projects in the world. Vince had been in a lousy mood for a couple of weeks now, and all because of the virgin-hunt. If it weren't for that, he'd be enjoying himself up here at the lake.

And, in the third and last place, it meant he was missing a lot of sure stuff. You go after a virgin, she's liable to still be a virgin after you leave her. You go after one that's been made before, you've got a better chance to make her again.

Three reasons, and all of them good ones. Vince spent a couple of days going over them, trying to talk himself out of this quest of the holy quail, then he strolled over to his father's car, slid behind the wheel, and drove off to see if this lousy lake could boast of even one single guaranteed virgin.

It could. Adele Christopher. And this time, he was absolutely sure. Never mind about appearances being deceiving, they couldn't be all that deceiving. Adele Christopher was a virgin, no question about it.

Actually, she wasn't much Vince's type. She was a short, slender, mousy girl, with a boyish figure. She had breasts, but they were about the size of a bee-bite. And she had hips, but just barely. She did have good legs, at least, and a pleasant, oval face beneath short-cropped mouse-blonde hair, and she was definitely a virgin.

Adele was sixteen, but she looked more like twelve. She usually wandered around wearing scuffed loafers and frayed faded blue jeans and a white man's shirt with the tails tied in a knot beneath her bee-bites. But her little butt wiggled nicely inside the tight blue jeans, and her waist looked small enough to put his arm completely around it, and she had a nice friendly smile and clear blue eyes.

She wasn't precisely his type, but the more he looked at her, the more he had a feeling she could become his type without too much trouble at all. There was an old saying he'd heard once: The closer to the bone, the sweeter the meat. And you couldn't get much closer to the bone than skinny Adele.

He'd also heard it said that a thin woman is built for speed and a fat woman is built for comfort. A girl like Adele, being as thin as that—and it would be her first time, too, of that he was sure—she might just go wild. It didn't take much thinking it over before he really began to look forward to the experience.

The first thing, of course, was to get to know the girl better. He'd met her at the grocery store-post office around on the north shore of the lake, talked with her a bit, seen her a few times when he'd swum from his own cabin to the public beach near the store, but it had never been any more than talk about the weather and sunburn and how cold the lake water was. So the first thing to do was get to know her better.

That part was easy enough. He drove around the lake to the store, parked in the gravel parking lot beside the store, and there she was, at the public beach, sitting with a bunch of girls. She was dressed, as usual, in blue jeans, white shirt and scuffed loafers, and she looked, as usual, not a day over twelve.

He went over and talked for a while, talking with the whole group of girls. The usual vacation-at-the-lake crap, about the weather and the temperature of the water and all that; and when the right moment came, he asked her if she wanted to join him for a coke over at the store. Adele wouldn't be a wine girl like Rhonda. She'd be a coke and hot dogs girl.

And, of course, her Dream Man would be a coke and hot dogs boy. An outdoorsy type, young and kind of gawky, the kind of clown who'd wander around with Lassie at his heels. So that was the way Vince played it, young and gawky and full of coke. He fooled around with the notion of borrowing a dog from somebody, but decided it was too much trouble, and he could be gawky enough all by himself.

She went with him for the coke, but so did two of the other girls. That was the thing with girls, particularly short fat ugly girls like the two who came along to share the coke. They always ran in packs. You get a bunch of good-looking girls together, it's no trouble at all to cull one out of the herd. You get a bunch of beasts together, with one good-looking girl in their midst, and they'll cling to the looker as though she were a life-preserver. Vince thought that was probably because they knew the looker would attract males, and they didn't want to miss out if there were any extras. Or maybe they were just hoping some of the looks would rub off on them if they hung around long enough.

He knew better than to let the girls know he was less than overjoyed to have them along. He knew he had to make believe he liked Adele's bug-eyed monster friends if he wanted to get anywhere with her. So he grinned at them and talked with them, and waited half an hour before asking Adele if she wanted to go for a ride around the lake. She said yes, and he pulled her away before the beasts knew what was going on.

That first day, all they did was drive around the lake, looking at the cabins and the swimmers and the motorboats, while Vince did some strong groundwork on the Dream Man. By the time he brought her back to the store, where she wanted to be let off, he knew he had her hooked. She thought he was just the greatest thing since Claude Jarman, Jr. "I'll see you tomorrow," he said as she got out of the car, and she smiled and nodded, looking very pleased.

He spent four days that way, just driving her around the lake, going swimming with her either at the public beach or the little beach behind his parents' cabin, and all the time building up the young and gawky impression for her.

After the first day, he didn't have too much trouble with the beasts any more. It was obvious that Adele preferred to go off with him, rather than hang around with the tons of fun, and that was an excellent sign. There was only one of the beasts who caused any trouble at all; a short, heavy, stringy-haired mound named Bobbi. She even managed, on the second day, to come along for the ride around the lake—which pleased Vince no end. After that, he worked extra hard to keep himself and Adele away from lovable old Bobbi.

The fourth day was a Friday, and there was to be a dance that night in Cornwallville, a town about eight miles from the lake. In a Grange Hall, no less. While they were driving around that afternoon, Vince asked her if she wanted to go to the dance with him, and she said she'd be glad to. By that time, they were old hound-dog buddies.

So that Friday night was the first real date. He knew he was dealing with a genuine virgin this time—there wasn't the slightest doubt of that at all, he kept telling himself—so he played it very cautious on their first date. At the dance, which was lousy, consisting of a hillbilly jukebox alternating with some local hillbilly non-talent, he danced with her as though they were brother and sister. Afterward, he drove her right back to her cabin, and kissed her only once before saying good-night. She was surprised that he hadn't tried to kiss her again, he could tell that, and he knew she wanted him to kiss her again. She could keep wanting for a little while, he told himself. Work the anticipation bit.

At first, he'd been planning the defloration for the backseat of his father's car, but as the time grew nearer, he began to think about the mechanics of the thing again; that business of switching from front seat to back, of squirming around trying to get your clothes off in a cramped backseat, and he decided a grassy slope somewhere under a tree would be a hell of a lot better all the way around.

But not out at the island. Not after the fiasco with Rhonda. He didn't want to have anything to do with that lousy island ever again. Somewhere else.

He took some time out to look for a new spot, a place as secluded and handy as the island. He went looking on Monday afternoon, three days after the dance.

The thing was, this was a vacation-type lake. Every inch of shore was used by somebody or other, with cabins and docks and boathouses and beaches. A two-lane blacktop road circled the lake, and even the side of the road away from the lake was solidly lined with cabins.

Yet he couldn't roam too far away from the lake. He had to find a spot close enough so it would seem natural to go there. It would be in the afternoon, of course. An outdoorsy girl like Adele, you could only de-virginize her in the daytime, with the sun shining like mad.

He drove around Monday afternoon, looking for a secluded spot and not finding one. Then he noticed the little stream that fed into the lake from the east, tumbling down from the wooded hills back of the lake. There was a small bridge at the point where the road crossed the stream, and he noticed what looked like a narrow path leading off from the road along the streamside.

He stopped the car just beyond the bridge and walked back to look at the stream and the path. There was nothing up that way but woods. No roads and no cabins and no people. The path was overgrown, barely visible more than a few feet from the road.

This looked like the place. It would be the most natural thing in the world for a nature boy like Vince to suggest a little walk up that path. And it would be the most natural thing in the world for a nature girl like Adele to think it a great idea.

But it might also be a great idea to check first, to make sure there was some sort of clearing up that way, someplace where a couple of nature-lovers could lie down and have some room, if they happened to feel like it.

Vince didn't like to walk, not even on sidewalks. And he especially didn't like to walk along overgrown and weed-choked paths in the God-forsaken great outdoors. But a man with a goal will suffer a lot of inconvenience to reach that goal. And Vince was definitely a man with a goal. He started walking.

The stream meandered around like an idiot, curving back and forth and climbing erratically over hills, and the path followed right next to it, occasionally angling away from the stream for a few yards to cut through some particularly heavy underbrush. Vince fought his way along, and the farther he got the more overgrown the woods became, with trees crammed closer and closer together and all kinds of bushes and weeds stuffed in among the trunks. It looked as though there was no such thing as a clearing in these lousy woods.

But there was. And it was inhabited.

He heard the voices first, ahead of him. They sounded familiar, but they were still some distance ahead, and he couldn't figure out who it was. He had a sudden fear that it might be Rhonda, and he almost turned around right then and ran back to the car.

But he didn't. The voices might mean there was an open space ahead. Vince left the path, climbing up a steep slope away from the stream, planning to circle around and see who these people were before showing himself to them.

He was halfway up the slope when he suddenly realized that one of the voices was Adele's. He hesitated, wondering what the hell Adele was doing there, and all at once he had the horrible fear that he'd goofed again; that not even Adele was a virgin, that she was up here with some guy.

Maybe there just wasn't any such thing as a virgin, after all. Maybe virgins were myths, like unicorns. He suddenly remembered the legend that only a virgin could capture a unicorn, and now he understood that legend. It took a myth to catch a myth.

But as he stood there thinking about it, getting more disgusted every second, the other voice started talking again and, with a sigh of relief, he realized the other voice also belonged to a girl. So Adele wasn't up here with a guy, after all. It was just one of her little Brownie friends.

He thought he heard Adele mention his name. Sure, she was talking about him, she was telling the Brownie about him. Good old Adele.

He wondered what she was saying about him. He moved forward even more slowly and cautiously now, wanting to get close enough to hear what Adele had to say.

From the top of the slope, he could see them. It was Adele and the tons of fun, Bobbi, the menace who'd been hanging around so much all last week.

And there was a clearing. A great clearing, right out of a storybook. It was oval in shape, with the stream gurgling through the middle of the oval the long way. There were level grassy banks right down to the edge of the stream, and the whole place was ringed with slender-trunked young trees and dark green shrubbery.

Adele and Bobbi were sitting on the grass next to the stream, on the same side as Vince. They were both dressed in the uniform of the area, blue jeans and white men's shirts, and they were sitting chatting together about one thing and another. And mainly about Vince.

He lay prone on his stomach on the top of the slope, peering through the high grass, and watched and listened.

Bobbi was saying, "Vince wants to make love to you, you know."

"Oh, don't be silly," said Adele. "All boys think about it, but it doesn't mean anything. I mean, he isn't going to try anything."

Vince grinned down the slope at Adele. That's what you think, little baby, he thought. And what a great big surprise you've got coming. A great big surprise.

"I know why you're going around with him so much," Bobbi was saying. "It's to make me mad."

"I haven't been going around with him so much," objected Adele, but she smiled at the other girl, and she didn't deny the charge. "We've just gone riding in his car, that's all, just riding around the lake."

"You went to the dance with him Friday night," Bobbi said. Vince could see now that Bobbi was pouting. There was accusation in her voice.

Adele shrugged. "I wanted to go to the dance," she said. "What's wrong with that? And I couldn't very well have gone with you."

"Why not?" Bobbi demanded. "Girls go to dances together all the time. They even dance together. Who'd think anything?"

"I don't know about your parents," Adele told her, "but my mother and father are beginning to suspect."

Vince frowned, not following the conversation at all. Suspect? Suspect what?

Oh for God's sake, he thought suddenly, they're members of a non-virgin club. He knew it, he knew it, he'd known it all along, there just wasn't any such thing as a virgin. Virgins and unicorns, mythical beasties.

The conversation was still going on down there, and through his depression Vince continued to listen, and what they were saying down there just kept getting more mystifying all the time.

"They do not," Bobbi was saying. "Parents never suspect a thing like that. We could do it right in front of them, for Pete's sake, and they'd think we were just playing games."

"All I know," Adele said, "is that Mom's been hinting that I ought to stay away from you. And every time she gets on the subject, she gets too embarrassed for words."

"Then don't worry about it," Bobbi advised her. "Even if they think they know something, what difference does it make if they're afraid to call you on it?"

"I don't think I'd want them to know," Adele said soberly.

"Are you ashamed? I told you, Adele, there's nothing in the world to be ashamed of. There've been lots and lots of women—"

"I know all that. I just don't want my parents to know about it, that's all."

"You changed the subject," said Bobbi suddenly. "You didn't want to talk about that Vince any more."

Adele smiled, and lay back on the grass, staring up at the sky. "I think I like him," she said thoughtfully.

"Adele, don't be mean."

"I think maybe I'll let him make love to me," she said, still smiling at the sky.

Vince sat up and took notice. Now, *that* was the kind of thing he liked to hear!

"Adele, you're just teasing me," Bobbi said reproachfully. "Don't tease me like that."

"I wonder how it would be," mused Adele, ignoring the other girl. "I wonder how it would be to have a man make love to me." She turned and looked at Bobbi, grinning wickedly at her. "Don't you wonder sometimes how it would feel?"

Bobbi made a face and said, "Ugh!"

"I do," said Adele. She lay back on the grass again. "And I think I really will do it. I'll bring Vince up here and—"

"Adele, stop it!"

"After all," Adele went on, "I really ought to try it."

She was a virgin, Vince was thinking gleefully. This time, for sure, she was a virgin.

She went on, saying, "Just once, of course. But I ought to try it once, see what it's like. Maybe I'd enjoy it."

Oh, you would, little baby, thought Vince. You sure as hell would. And you sure as hell *will*.

"I think I'd like him to—"

"*Stop!*" Bobbi, her face contorted with rage, suddenly lunged forward and cracked Adele ringingly across the face, open-handed. "Stop that!" she screamed. "Stop tormenting me like that!"

"Don't you slap *me!*" Adele was suddenly enraged, too, and came up from the grass swinging.

Vince stared at them in blank-faced astonishment. Their conversation, their actions—none of it made any sense. And now they were rolling around on the ground down there, punching and scratching and biting each other, and he couldn't figure out for the life of him just what the hell they were fighting about.

The two of them, fighting grimly and silently now, kept rolling around on the grass, slugging and clawing one another, until finally the inevitable happened, and they both tumbled off the bank and into the shallow stream.

They came up gurgling and thrashing, and all at once they weren't fighting any more. They looked at one another, solemnly, and both climbed back out of the stream, and sat down on the bank once more.

They sat in silence for a while, Vince watching and scratching his head, until at last Adele said, softly, "I'm sorry I teased you, Bobbi. I shouldn't be mean like that."

"And I'm sorry I slapped you," Bobbi said. "But when you talk that way, I just get so jealous I can't stand it. And when you keep going off with that Vince all the time—"

"I won't do that anymore," said Adele. "I'm really and truly sorry, Bobbi."

Vince blinked. What was this? A minute ago, she'd been talking about making it with him. Now she was saying she wasn't even going to go for rides with him anymore. He wondered what the hell was going on down there, and he also wondered just who in hell Bobbi thought she was, and where she came off, queering his deal that way.

Bobbi got to her feet, a round blob in the middle of the clearing. "My clothes are soaked," she said.

"Mine, too." Adele stood up beside her, and started undoing her shirt. "We better take them off and spread them out on the grass, so they'll dry."

"What if somebody sees us?" And Bobbi looked up the slope, straight at where Vince was hiding. Even though he knew it was impossible for her to see him, he winced and ducked lower into the grass.

"Nobody ever comes up here," Adele said offhandedly, and she stripped off her shirt. She was wearing a bra beneath it, which was a waste of good money. Those bee-bites of hers didn't need any support at all. She spread the shirt on the grass, then removed the bra, and her breasts barely cast a shadow.

Bobbi, still a little hesitant, also stripped off her wet clothes. Vince looked at them both, and he thought they really should have been cut closer to the middle of the deck. Where Adele was thin as a rail, with breasts smaller than the White Rock girl, and hips skinnier than a basketball player's; Bobbi was busting out all over. She had breasts that could have been used for sandbags, and a butt that was a sandbag. Nothing else in the world could be that wide and round and saggy.

They were both nude before it occurred to him that his status had just changed from eavesdropper, which wasn't really very bad, to peeping tom, which was very bad. He ought to get away from there before they found him and got the wrong idea.

But he was afraid to move, afraid he might make some small sound that they would hear. And now, with their clothes off, they'd be more alert for the sounds of other people. So he stayed where he was, and waited for a chance to slip away.

Besides, it was pleasant to have a preview of Adele's body. The legs, as he'd already known, were very good, with strong and supple thighs and good calves. And her stomach was flat, her waist delicate and tiny. The bee-bite breasts weren't much, but it might be fun to play with them a bit. Play delicately, of course, in relation to their size. Just with fingers, not with the whole hand.

Now stripped, Adele lay on her back, one arm across her eyes to keep out the sun, one knee raised. Vince nodded approvingly. That's the position, little baby, he thought. You just keep practicing that.

And then Bobbi's hand reached out and squeezed Adele's breast.

Vince blinked. What the hell was that all about?

He'd expected Adele to sit up like a shot, hollering, but she didn't do anything of the kind. Instead, she smiled and murmured, and reached up to press Bobbi's hand tighter against her breast.

"I do love you so," Bobbi said, and her voice was so soft that Vince could barely make out the words. "You know how much I love you. You shouldn't tease me the way you do."

"I know, honey," Adele said soothingly. She smiled up at Bobbi contritely and said, "I won't do that any more."

Bobbi leaned down and kissed Adele on the lips, and Adele's arms twined around the other girl, and soon they were lying side by side on the grass, stroking each other's body and murmuring.

After the first movement by Bobbi, Adele became the aggressor of the two. Bobbi lay flat on her back, and Adele leaned over her, stroking her breasts and stomach and thighs, kissing her, leaning down to nip at her breasts, kissing all over Bobbi's body.

When they really got into it, and Vince knew they wouldn't be paying any attention to outside sounds for a while, he crept slowly back down the slope, and headed down the path for the road and his car. He kept shaking his head in disgusted amazement, and trying to figure out what the hell kind of world it was he was living in anyway.

Well, he'd found his virgin. There was no getting around that, he'd found a guaranteed virgin. Guaranteed for life.

And that, he told himself, was definitely that. First two phonies, and now a dyke. Talk about queering the deal! Okay, the virgin-hunt was off. He was cured.

Back at the road, he got into the car and drove toward home. The virgin-hunt was off, and he was soured on the lake. He didn't want to be at any lake with Rhonda and Adele—the relationship kid and the dyke. He didn't know for sure where he did want to be, but he did know for sure he didn't want to be at the lake.

His father was reading the paper, inevitably, on the screened-in porch of the cabin. Vince went into his bedroom, which had a window looking out onto the porch, and grabbed his suitcase. As he stuffed clothes into it, he said through the window to his father, "You aren't going to be needing the car for about a week, are you?"

His father looked up from the paper, startled. "What?"

His suitcase packed, Vince said, "I'd like to take off in the car for about a week. You don't need it, do you?"

"Well—well, no. But—"

"Okay if I take it for a week? Don't worry, I won't crack it up or anything."

"I know that," his father said. "You're a good driver, Vince. But—"

"Then it's okay, huh?"

"Well, I suppose so, but—"

"Fine." He grabbed the suitcase and left the bedroom.

His father followed, the paper trailing from his hand. "Where are you going?"

Vince dumped the suitcase into the backseat of the car, slid behind the wheel, said, "See you in a week," and took off.

Chapter 4

The trouble with just pointing the car and heading down the road was that you might just happen to wind up in Brighton. And it wasn't easy to imagine a worse place than Brighton. Even the cruddy cabin by the cruddy lake, rustically rotten as it was, would have been better. Except, of course, for charmers like Rhonda and Adele.

The combination of Relationship Rhonda and Dykey Adele made it necessary to head for greener pastures. But Brighton wasn't exactly greener pastures. It was more on the order of a desert.

It was so simple at first, Vince thought. You got in the car, stepped on the gas, and drove. When you found a quarry worth pursuing, then you stopped.

Sure you did.

The problems occurred after you were heading down the old road. There were plenty of problems. For one thing, you didn't know where the hell you were going. For another thing, you had to get the damned car back to the damned cabin in a week, maybe ten days at the outside. That sort of ruled out a trip to any town that might be worth going to.

This limited things. He couldn't go to Florida, which might have been nice, and he couldn't go to California, which also might have been nice, and he couldn't go to Alaska, which might have been even nicer. But he still could have gone to New York, or Philadelphia, or Boston. New York, in some small way, meant Rhonda, which was disturbing, but Boston or Philadelphia would have been one hell of a lot better than Brighton.

Brighton.

But there was one more problem, one overwhelming problem, and the problem was money. More precisely, the lack of money. He had fifty dollars and change with him when he took off, and while fifty dollars was a small fortune when you lived with your folks, fifty dollars was very little when it was the sole support of both yourself and a car.

A hungry car. A car that, with a good tailwind, managed ten miles to the gallon. A car that drank oil like a Bowery bum with a thing for petroleum. A car that could easily burn up fifty dollars getting to Boston or Philadelphia or New York.

The smart thing to do was to turn back and give it up as a bad job. But that meant Rhonda, and Adele, and more than anything else it meant admitting defeat.

So he did the dumb thing—which meant Brighton.

He pushed the car seventy miles down the road, passing two towns even worse than Brighton, towns consisting of a gas pump and a general store and three empty houses. And then he reached Brighton, which had more empty houses and two general stores and an occasional hitching post. It was about time either to fill the gas tank or park the car. So he parked the car. It was cheaper.

He had a plan. The plan was the essence of simplicity. He would get the cheapest room he could find, eat the cheapest meals he could stomach, and lay the prettiest girl in the town.

Not a virgin, and not a dyke, and not an Uninhibited Relationship. A girl, an ordinary girl. There had to be at least one pretty girl in Brighton, for God's sake.

So he got a room, a cubbyhole in a white frame Rooms-For-Rent run by a gray-headed keep-smiling tub of lard named Mrs. Rebecca Sharp. The room was fifteen dollars a week with meals, and by the looks of Mrs. Sharp, she could cook well. The room was clean, the meals turned out fine, and money was a little less of a problem.

And then, all settled, he went on the hunt for the prettiest girl in Brighton. And found her.

Her name was Saralee Jenkins and she was beautiful. Her face was the best part, sort of along the lines of a small-town Grace Kelly, with long blonde hair and blue eyes and an occasional freckle on her nose. The body was good, too. Not quite as good as Rhonda, maybe, but a hell of a lot better than Adele the Dyke. She was kind of short, with well-established breasts and a very slim waist, with legs that were damned fine up to the knee and probably better and better as they went along.

And she was not a virgin. If anybody was not a virgin, she was not a virgin. No virgin looked at you in quite that way. No virgin moved her tail in quite that manner when she walked down the street. There might be a virgin somewhere in the civilized world, but this was definitely not the one.

She worked behind the counter at the drugstore, making sodas and sundaes for the local yokels and frying an occasional greasy hamburger for an occasional greasy kid. Vince saw her for the first time when he stopped in for a coke, and he knew right away that this was the girl; that she was the only one in Brighton worth bothering with, that she was fair game, and that she was not a virgin. This last point he knew instinctively, and later he found it out for certain.

And this was part of the problem. In fact, it was the problem, plain and simple.

She was married.

There were a few rules in the quail-hunting game, and one of them was that you did not fool around with a married woman. You just didn't. All you got out of it was trouble, and occasionally you got killed, and it just wasn't worth it. Vince had had enough opportunities in the past, and once or twice he had been genuinely tempted, but each time his guns had remained in his holster and the prize had not been shot down. There were women in Modnoc, available women, and they had made their availability obvious. But he had pictured himself in the saddle when the horse's owner walked into the room, and he had quietly forgotten the women involved.

But this was different.

For one thing, Saralee was too damned willing to play. That message hit him the minute he saw her, even before he saw the gold band on her finger. The way she looked at him, and the way she talked to him, and everything else about her—she was just there to be had.

Which was bad.

What was worse was that he wanted her, wanted her badly. The Adele episode had left him badly shaken. He needed a girl now, and without one he might go quietly mad. And the rest of the available talent in Brighton was either ugly or virginal. Saralee was neither.

He wanted her and she wanted him. And meanwhile her jerk of a husband, old Bradley Jenkins, stood in the back of the store filling prescriptions. That was all the dumb son-of-a-bitch seemed to know how to do. There was Saralee, itching for love, and the moron was filling prescriptions. It was ridiculous.

He talked with her for about half an hour the first day. She kept dropping hints and he pretended to be too dumb to see what she was getting at, which would have been very dumb indeed. Then, miraculously, the coke was gone, and he had a chance to leave.

So he did.

He spent the rest of the day trying to find someone else to spend the week with, but there wasn't anyone. The girls who had looked merely beastly at first, now looked downright nauseating. He walked all over town, which took all of fifteen minutes, and the more he walked and the more girls he looked at, the worse they looked and the better Saralee looked.

He got back to Mrs. Sharp's just in time for supper, which didn't taste as good this day as it had the day before. He didn't feel much like eating. He felt being alone, and after dinner he went to his room and stretched out on the bed.

There were so many reasons to stay away from Saralee Jenkins. Fine reasons. But the more he thought about them, the less important they became. There were other reasons, reasons why he should crawl between Saralee's anxious arms as soon as possible; and these reasons grew bigger and loomed larger and more significant the more he pondered them.

She was hungry for it, that was for sure. Her broken-down excuse for a husband wasn't doing his job. She needed a young man, and he needed her, and that was that.

She would be good. She would be damned good and hungry the way she was, hungry for him. It was good to have principles, and staying away from married women was a good principle to have, but there was a limit. She was worth stepping out of line for.

More important, it wasn't as if he was crapping in his own backyard. Nobody knew him in Brighton. He could creep up on her like a thief in the night, get what he'd come for, and then head back to the little cabin on the lake. That would be the end of her and the end of Brighton, and to hell with both of them.

He still didn't like it. Either way he didn't like it. Staying in Brighton without sleeping with her would be impossible, and creeping back to the lake with his tail between his legs would be unbearable, and heading onward and downward to still another hick town in the middle of nowhere would be even worse.

And, in the meantime, the second day was drawing to an uneventful close. There were just five more days, and then it was back to the lake, which meant he didn't have a hell of a lot of time to play games. Five days to get in and get out and go home.

The first thing to do, he told himself, was to relax. He counted his money, decided he couldn't really afford to see a movie but that he was going to do so anyway.

The price was a pleasant half a buck, which was a break, but the movie was a western, which wasn't. He sat through it, sighed with relief when it was over, and headed back to the room to sack out.

Before he went to sleep, his mind was made up. He was going to drop over to the drugstore the next afternoon. If anything happened, it happened. If nothing happened, nothing happened.

He drifted off to sleep hoping desperately that something would happen.

Something happened. It was a few minutes after two when he strolled into the drugstore, took a stool at the counter and ordered a coke. She gave him, in addition to the coke, a huge grin and a quick wink that was about as subtle as a blasting cap. When she shoved the coke at him she managed to lean so far over the counter that her uniform dropped about five inches away from her breasts. The breasts had looked damned good with the uniform around them and looked even better all by themselves. He tried to look away, but it wasn't easy.

"Like what you see?"

He stared at her.

"Because if you do—"

A customer came in and mercifully cut the discussion short before it really got going. The customer was a middle-aged woman with a pot belly who had the gall to order a double banana split with extra whipped cream. It took Saralee awhile to slap the garbage together, and while she was splitting bananas and scooping ice cream he tried to pull himself together.

She wasn't just forward. She was brazen, and eager, and ready. It wasn't a quail hunt, not this time. It was a rooster hunt. She was the one who was doing the hunting, and he was the one who was being hunted, and somehow this took the joy of the chase out of it.

But, at the same time...

It took the woman a lot less time to devour the double banana split than it had taken Saralee to prepare it. The sloppy old broad waddled out of the drugstore and off into the wilds of Brighton, and there they were again.

He felt trapped.

"He's old and he's ugly and he's no good," she was telling him. "And you're young and fresh and I want you. How old are you, Vince?"

"Seventeen."

"Is that all?"

"That's all."

"Most boys your age would have said they were older than that."

He shrugged. If she thought he was going to lie about his age just for a chance at her fair young body, she had another think coming.

"I never lie," he lied.

"I'm only nineteen," she said. "I guess it's all right. I mean, I'm two years older than you, but it doesn't make much difference. You're probably pretty mature for your age, anyway."

Sure, he thought. But only below the neck.

"And he's forty-three," she said, nodding in the direction of the prescription department. "Forty-three years old and no damn good at all. You know what it's like for a girl with a man like that?"

"Must be rough."

She nodded. "It's horrible."

He took a breath. "Look," he said. "I mean, there must be guys in town. You shouldn't have any trouble."

"That's just it, Vince. I'm not a tramp. If I did it with anybody from Brighton it would be all over town. Don't you see? But you're from out of town and nobody would have to know. We would just do it and it would be great and then it would be over."

"I guess I'm the answer to a maiden's prayers."

She leaned close, giving him another look at her navel. "I'm no maiden," she said. "But you're the answer. You got a car?"

"Sort of."

"Listen to me. You pick me up on the corner of Fourth and Schwerner at seven-thirty. We'll be done with dinner by then and I'll tell him I'm going out for a walk. But I won't be going for a walk. I'll be going for a ride, and then we'll stop the car, and then well both be going for a ride again. You understand?"

"Seven-thirty," he said stupidly.

"That's right. You'll be there, won't you? Because I'll be waiting."

"I guess so."

"You sound afraid. You're not afraid of me, are you? I don't think you're afraid. I'll bet you've had lots of girls. I'll bet you're real good at it."

"Don't worry," he advised her. "I'm not a virgin. There aren't any."

For a minute she looked bewildered, which was understandable. Then she did another deep knee bend and showed him her chest again.

"Look what I've got," she said. "All for you. And more, all for you. Anything you want, and it's all for you, Vince. Don't keep me waiting."

You're not afraid of me, are you?

Hell, no. Not him. He wasn't afraid. He was going to pick her up, and take her for a drive, and give her a workout that would keep her happy for the next hundred years. And then he would get back in the car and point the car away from Brighton and that would be that. Afraid? What in hell was there to be afraid of?

He was scared stiff.

He didn't taste dinner. But he finished it, somehow, and by seven-fifteen he was in the car. He drove to the gas station, put a couple bucks worth in the tank, and headed toward Schwerner Street. He drove along Schwerner to Second, and then to Third, and all the way he kept half-hoping that he would get to Fourth and she wouldn't be there.

She was, of course. He stopped the car and she was sitting next to him at once, her lips already parted for a kiss. His tongue darted between the lips and her arms wound around him and that chest of hers pressed tight against him. And then he wasn't scared any more.

"I couldn't wait," she said. "I thought you wouldn't come and I thought somebody might see us and I thought I would go out of my mind. But you came and nobody saw us and it's all right now. Take a right turn, there's an old road a few miles up. Nobody ever goes there. We'll be all right."

He couldn't talk. He just drove, finding the old road, wondering absently how many other guys had taken her there, then stopping the car and not wondering or caring about anything but Saralee.

The chase was gone, but there was something far more exciting in its own way than the chase. There was a woman, a woman born for love, and there was Vince, and the two of them were getting along fine.

The old awkwardness of seduction in an automobile didn't come into the picture, not when the girl involved was so eager to be seduced. He was happily surprised when Saralee scampered over the seat and into the back the minute the brakes were on.

From there on it was ideal. He didn't have to undress her because she began tearing her own clothes off instantly. He had all he could do to get his own clothes off fast enough. Then she was in his arms, and she was kissing him again, and all of her was next to all of him.

"Sooooooo good, Vince. Touch me here and here and here. Touch me all over, touch me, kiss me, bite me, do everything to me. Don't ever stop, Vince. Please don't stop. I don't want it to stop. I want it to go on forever. Please, Vince. Oh, it's so good. So good, Vince, and I need it so much, and yes I need it, Vince, yes it's so good don't yes don't stop keep going yes I love it yes I love it yes I love it I need it I want it oh yes yes yes yes YES!"

It was over, suddenly, and the uncomfortable feeling of having been seduced was overridden by the joy of having been seduced so expertly. There was no getting around it—some girls were a lot better at it than other girls. And when a girl was good at it, and wanted it, it made a difference. One hell of a difference.

Of course, the car wasn't the best place in the world. It was cramped, even an old boat of a car like his father's. And it must have inhibited her performance, as good old Rhonda would have put it. Not that Saralee seemed at all inhibited, not in the least. But the poor girl didn't have enough room to move around in.

And she loved to move. Oh, how she loved to move. And she moved so nicely.

"Vince—"

He cupped one of her breasts and gave it a friendly squeeze.

"Vince, I needed that. You have no idea how much I needed that. It's been so long."

"Look," he said, "I don't want to get personal, but what the hell's wrong with your husband? Is he dead or something?"

"He's no good."

"Well . . . doesn't he even try?"

She giggled. "Once a night," she said. "Once a night, every goddamned night of the year."

He gaped. "Isn't once a night enough for you?"

"Well," she said, giggling, "to begin with, it isn't. Not tonight, anyway, because we're going to do it again as soon as I get my wind back."

"But—"

"Ordinarily, once a night would be enough. Once with you, for example, would be plenty. But Brad gets through before I even get started. All he does is get me the least bit hot and it's over and I have to crawl up the walls."

"Oh," he said.

"And I can't stand it, because I need it, and you came along and I knew you'd be good. And you are good, Vince. You're wonderful. You're the best ever."

"Well," he said. "Thanks."

"And we're going to do it again," she said. "Right here and right now, but we'll have to hurry a little so he doesn't get suspicious. We'll have to start right now, so get set, honey. Because we're going to do it and it's going to be great.

"Now," she said. "Now, yes, now, Vince, now!"

It was too soon, and he was tired, but she was persuasive.

Very persuasive.

And very skillful.

So skillful, in fact, that when in the course of things he pulled a small muscle in his back he didn't even notice it until later.

And it was worth it, anyway.

There was always the smart thing and the dumb thing, and it was beginning to seem as though the dumb thing was whatever he did. Or, rather, whatever the dumb thing was, he picked it.

Maybe he was just dumb.

Because, if he was smart, he would have gotten the hell out of Brighton the minute he dropped Saralee on the corner of Schwerner and Fourth. The game was won, the trophy would look good on the wall, and that was that.

But he wasn't smart.

He stayed the night at Mrs. Sharp's. That was dumb, of course, but it was also natural. He was just too damned tired to drive all the way back to the lake without a good night's sleep first.

Besides, he'd paid up for a whole week. He might as well collect a night's sleep there and breakfast in the morning before he left.

Sure.

That, he told himself in the morning, was not exactly the truth. Vince, boy, you're not being honest with yourself. You don't give a lily-white damn about breakfast in the morning. You're wondering what Sexy Saralee would be like in a real bed.

Which was something he didn't have any right to think about.

For one thing, once with Saralee was enough. Twice with Saralee had almost been fatal, albeit wonderful, and a third time would be dangerous.

On the way to the drugstore, he told himself it was just to see her, to say good-bye. No sense running out without even telling her so long.

Uh-huh.

"Tonight," she said. "Tonight, Vince. Again tonight, and not in the car because it's better in a bed. Tonight we'll do it in a bed, Vince.

"Brad works late tonight," she went on. "You come over to my house and we'll do it and it'll be perfect, just perfect. In my bed. It's a big double bed and we'll have loads of room. You'll like it, Vince."

That sounded entirely possible.

"169 Hayes Street," she said. "Right on the corner of Fifth. Come up at eight o'clock and it'll give us two hours before he gets home. You come right up, Vince. You understand?"

He understood. Boy, did he understand. He understood so well he wanted to crawl in a hole.

"Look," he said, "Saralee, I mean, I have to get back home and—"

"Hush up," she said. "You better go now. I'll see you tonight."

So I'm stupid, he thought. So I'm a damned fool who ought to know better. So I'm a low-grade moron with a rock for a head. So what?

He parked the car around the corner from her house, then listened to his knees banging together on the way to her door. He rang the bell once, wondering what in God's name he would do if her husband answered the door, and then listened to his teeth chattering until she came to the door and opened it. She was stark naked.

He stood there, just staring, and then he managed to step inside and get the door shut.

"Jesus Christ," he said. "I mean, that's pretty stupid, Saralee. Suppose it wasn't me at the door, for God's sake. Suppose—"

"I saw you," she said. "From the window."

"But—"

"So I knew it was you and not somebody else. I didn't want to waste any time. I still don't want to waste any time. I want to get started, because we only have two hours, and I want to make the most of both of them. What's the matter? Don't you like the way I look?"

He couldn't answer. All he could do was look at her. Most girls, he had learned long ago, look a lot better with some clothes on. And a naked girl who was just sort of lying down looked a lot better than one walking around. But Saralee was an exception.

She was perfect naked, perfect the way she wandered around without seeming conscious of the fact that she was nude.

She was lovely.

"Hurry," she was saying. "The bedroom is upstairs, and we want to go there right away, and you'd better hurry."

They hurried.

In the bedroom, with the door shut, she helped him get his clothes off. She really wasn't much help. Every time she touched him he got confused and fumbled with his clothing, but finally he managed it and they were both naked.

And both on the bed.

She was telling him to hurry up, that she couldn't wait, that she'd been going out of her mind all day waiting for him.

But this time he was going to play it the way he wanted to.

"You're going to wait," he told her. "I'm going to drive you out of your mind."

And he spent a lot of time kissing and touching her, and pretty soon she was squirming and moaning for him, making strange sounds from somewhere in the depths of her throat and begging him to hurry, for God's sake, to get the main event started and stop wasting time on the preliminaries, to hurry up because she was going mad.

It was time. His point was proved, and she had learned her lesson, and now he did not feel that he was the one being seduced. This time it would be good, and when he finally did get the hell out of Brighton this would be something to remember.

"Come on," she said. "Vince, please. I'll kill you, Vince. I'll kill myself. I'll go mad. I can't take it, you better start doing it and stop fooling around. I want it, Vince, I need it. Vince, please—"

He got ready, and was about to begin, and then he noticed that she wasn't talking any more, that she wasn't saying a word, that she was looking past him with something horrible in her eyes.

So he looked around.

And there, big as life, was Bradley Jenkins.

Chapter 5

It was quite a tableau. There was Saralee Jenkins, flat upon her lovely back and reaching up with curving fingers for Vince. And there was Vince, naked as a jaybird, lowering himself to those waiting arms.

And there was Bradley Jenkins, standing in the doorway and staring at them both.

The next second just went on and on, while everybody stared at everybody else. And then that second was over, the next second had started, and everybody was in motion. Saralee gave a shriek and squirmed into a little ball, in a silly attempt to cover herself. Vince dove for his pants, on the chair beside the bed.

And Bradley Jenkins fell over in a faint.

That surprised Vince so much he missed the chair and went sailing into the wall. He clambered around, knocking things over, and when he got his balance and his footing back, he looked over at the door to be sure he'd seen right. Because he couldn't possibly have seen right. The husband who catches his wife in bed with another guy can do any number of things, from gunning the two of them down on the spot, through beating the guy up, to racing for his lawyer. But the one thing he doesn't do is faint.

But there was Bradley Jenkins on his face, passed out cold.

Vince thought fast. That was one thing he could do at least, he could think fast. And it was a good thing, because one thing he couldn't do was stay out of trouble.

The thoughts went flashing through his mind as he pulled his pants on. Number one, the husband was unconscious. Number two, he'd seen Vince for only a second, while in a state of shock, and while looking primarily at his wife, so he probably wouldn't even remember very clearly what Vince looked like. Not his face, anyway. Number three, if he moved fast enough he could get the hell out of here before the husband woke up again, and be out of town before Bradley Jenkins could figure out just what the hell was going on. Number four, Saralee knew his name, but she didn't know where he was from. Nobody in town did, not even Mrs. Sharp.

Which meant, number five, that with a little bit of luck and a lot of speed, he could get away with nothing worse than a bad scare.

Pants, shirt and shoes went on, and the rest of his clothes got stuffed into pockets. Then he jumped over the unconscious hubby and headed for the door.

Saralee grabbed him by the elbow as he was going through the doorway, swinging him around and practically slamming his nose into the jamb. She'd been busy, too, and was wearing blouse and skirt and loafers. "Take me with you!" she cried, and her eyes were wide with desperation.

"But—but—" He tried to slow down long enough to figure out the question, and the answer to it. "Your husband," he said.

"I'm through with him," she said. "I've been wanting to get out of this town for years. Take me with you."

"But—I'm only going home." The thought of going back to the lake, walking in to his mother and father, pointing to Saralee and saying, "She followed me home, can I keep her?" was a very strange one indeed.

She came up against him like a vibrating pad, jabbing him with the controls. "You don't have to go home," she said, seductively. "You can go anywhere you want, with that car of yours. And you could take me with you. We could go to New York." She vibrated some more. "We'd have a great time, Vince."

"But—I don't have any money. I don't have enough money to go to New York."

"Don't you worry about money, Vince," she said. She smiled and kissed him, and the vibrations got stronger and stronger. "Don't you worry about a thing, baby."

So there they were in Vince's car, driving hell for leather out of town. Saralee Jenkins, shed of her husband, sat very close beside him on the front seat. Vince's suitcase was in back, and so was Saralee's hastily packed overnight bag, and so was Saralee's bulging purse. The purse was stuffed with bills, ones and fives and tens and an occasional twenty, taken from hiding places all over the Jenkins house. "He didn't think I knew where he hid all this stuff," she'd said, grinning wickedly. "Brad underestimated me in every way, he did."

And now they were heading southeast in Vince's car, and Vince was having some second thoughts. Some very gloomy second thoughts.

What the hell is the use, he wondered, of being able to think fast in an emergency, if all of your thinking simply throws you pell-mell swell-hell into another emergency? No use, that's what use.

Question: Is it better to be caught by a husband with that husband's wife, or is it better to be caught by the police with the husband's wife and the husband's money? Don't answer.

It had all seemed so easy at the time, so simple and clear. Vince wasn't in any hurry to go back to Lake Lousy, and here was a chance for a trip to New York, all expenses paid, with a hot and willing female tossed in as an extra premium. Not an offer to pass up. That's the way it had seemed at the time.

So now Vince drove southeast through the night, and every pair of headlights reflected in the rear-view mirror shouted COP and every pair of headlights that shone through the windshield shouted TROOPER and Vince was beginning to get very very nervous.

Not Saralee, though. She wasn't worried at all. In fact, she was snuggling beside him and telling him all about her life in Brighton, and how she had happened to get tied up with a clunk like Bradley Jenkins.

"It seemed like such a good idea at the time," she was saying. "Mom was always after me about security, about how I shouldn't marry some randy bum who wouldn't support me. I should find some nice steady guy. And Brad had had the hots for me from the time I was fourteen and just beginning to push out my sweaters. So when I found out I was pregnant, two summers ago, and I wasn't sure who'd done it—and none of the possibilities would have made very good husbands—it seemed like a hell of a good idea to marry Brad. Security, you know, and a steady income, and a name for the kid."

"I didn't know you had a kid," Vince said. More complications, he thought. I'm not only stealing a wife from her husband, I'm stealing a mother from her child.

But Saralee said, "I don't." She curled her lip. "That's what made me so goddamn mad," she said. "I had a miscarriage two months after I got married. So I didn't even have to marry the old jerk after all."

"Oh," Vince said. Well, that was a relief. Vince felt he was due for some relief.

Apparently, so did Saralee, for she suddenly said, "You know, we never did finish what we set out to do."

"I know," said Vince. At the moment, he wasn't thinking about things like that. He was thinking that the more distance he put between himself and Brighton, the better off he was going to be.

"Boy, you know how to get a girl ready." She rubbed herself against him, and nibbled on his earlobe a little.

"Hey," he said. "I'm driving."

"Well, stop driving," she said, reasonably.

"I don't know if we ought to take the chance."

"Don't be silly. Brad doesn't know who you are, or what kind of car you've got, or where we're going or anything."

"Yeah, well—"

"You know," she said, "I got dressed so fast back there I didn't even have time to put on a bra or panties or anything. See?" She pulled her skirt up.

He saw. And he saw the light gleaming in her eyes, and he saw her hand reaching out for him, and he knew if he didn't stop the car pretty soon he'd run it off the road and into a tree. "Hold on," he said desperately. "Wait'll I find a side road or something."

"Hurry," she whispered, and her hands were not a devil's workshop.

Driving all over the road, Vince managed to turn left onto a side road, jounce off among the trees, stop the car and turn the engine off.

"I did so want to do it in a bed," she sighed. "But it's all right this way. It's all right anyway, just so we do it."

"I think I've got a blanket in the trunk," he said, surprised to find himself out of breath, as though he'd been running. "That'll be better than the backseat, anyway."

"Hurry," she whispered again.

He hurried. He clambered out of the car, opened the trunk and found the blanket. It was pretty dirty, but one side of it was clean. He spread it out on the ground beside the car, turned around, and she was naked again.

"Slowpoke," she said, grinning, and wriggled.

"You spend half your life without any clothes on," he said.

Vince, too, had dressed in too much of a hurry to be wearing much. So there wasn't much to take off. And then he was lying on the blanket beside her, and all at once he wasn't worried about anything any more. He was enjoying the sight of this woman, enjoying in advance what they were going to be doing together. "Now, let's see," he said, grinning at her. "Where were we?"

"You know damn well where we were," she said. "Come on."

"That's right," he said. "I was warming you up."

"I was all warmed," she said quickly. "I'm all warm now. Come on!"

"No, no," he said, and his hand stroked her breasts. "Gotta be warmer."

"Oh, don't go through all that again, Vince. Come on!"

"In a minute."

He forced himself to wait. While he stroked her and kissed her and squeezed her and fondled her, while she clawed at him and shrieked at him and pulsated for him, he forced himself to wait just as long as he could. He wanted her, he wanted her so bad that if Bradley Jenkins had shown up again, this time he would have kept right on going.

He stopped waiting. Vince thought this was surely it, they were going to kill themselves this way, the human body wasn't meant for this sort of punishment.

And then they were punching each other, screaming and snarling, kicking and biting, hurting one another and loving to hurt, loving to be hurt, and there they were, doing it again.

When it was over for the second time, Vince was exhausted. He just lay pillowed on her flat stomach and her lush breasts, with her warm breath in his ear and her hands, gentle now, caressing his back.

He dozed for a while, and woke up to hear her whispering, "You're getting heavy, Vince." Then he rolled off her, and they lay quietly side by side for a while. He fumbled for his clothes, found his cigarettes, lit one for her and one for himself, and they smoked quietly, resting, nude on the blanket among the trees.

"I'm glad you came along, Vince," she said finally. "I've wanted to get away from that stupid town for I don't know how long. But I never had the guts to do it before."

Vince didn't answer her. He was thinking about the fact that he had to bring the car back to the lake in only four more days. He wondered if he should tell Saralee about that, or if he should just go along with the gag, and quietly disappear four days from now.

It wasn't that he was worried about how she'd make out in New York after he left. A girl like Saralee, he knew there wasn't a thing to worry about. She'd make out fine in New York.

So, there really wasn't any need to tell her about anything. If he told her he was going to be leaving in four days, she would either try to talk him into staying, or she'd start looking early for somebody else to pal around with. If she tried to talk him into staying, using that body of hers as the main argument, she just might succeed, and then Vince would be in dutch with his old man. And if she started looking for somebody else the minute she got to New York, she'd find somebody else right away, and Vince would be out in the cold.

So he didn't tell her anything. Instead, he sat up and said, "I suppose we ought to get going."

"I suppose so," she said. She sat up and looked at him. "I don't suppose you could do it again," she said.

"Not without eight hours sleep, three pounds of steak, five raw eggs and a quart of milk," he told her. "And even then, I might not be in top form. You're an awful lot of woman, Saralee."

She smiled, murmuring, "Aren't I, though?" She threw her arms around him and kissed him. "There," she said. "To remember me by until you've got that sleep and steak and everything."

"Yeah," he said. He had the feeling it was going to be a hectic four days in New York.

This time they put on all their clothes. Then they climbed into the car, Vince backed it to the highway, and they set off again for New York.

She slept most of the trip, and Vince was just as pleased. He'd heard before of people with one-track minds, but this girl had a one-track body as well. When she was awake, there was only one thing she seemed to think of. She didn't need a man, she needed a platoon. She'd do fine in New York, Saralee would. She'd do great.

New York City at six in the morning of an already hot summer day doesn't look very much like Paradise. It looks and feels more like the other place. The streets are cluttered with papers and taxicabs and sweating human beings. The buildings are soot-darkened, the sky is a glaring white, the air is heavy with fumes and soot and humidity and the smell of eight million people.

Nevertheless, Vince was glad to see the George Washington bridge recede behind him. He'd been driving all night, after some pretty exhausting calisthenics, and he was ready for those eight hours sleep he'd been talking about. He prodded Saralee awake and said, "We're here. Now what?"

"Now," she said, "you park the car somewhere and we go find a hotel room."

Easier said than done, Vince thought. There was no place in New York to park a car, except the parking garages, where you had to pay. He told her so, and she said, "That's okay. I've got the money, remember?"

So they parked the car. Saralee did all the talking to the attendant at the garage, paying for a week's parking. "We won't need a car in New York," she explained to Vince, and he nodded, beginning to feel a little dirty for keeping silent about having to leave in four days.

Then they went to find a hotel. There was a convention in town, Vince learned at the first place they went to, and all the midtown hotels were full. The desk clerk suggested he try some of the hotels up around Broadway in the West Seventies. Vince thanked him, and they grabbed a cab, which Saralee paid for.

They found a hotel, finally, at Broadway and 72nd. Saralee had her wedding ring on, and they both had suitcases, and they were signing in for a week, so there was no trouble. Vince hesitated over the register, not knowing what name to put down, and then remembered a cat his Aunt Edith had once owned. So he put the cat's name down. "Mr. and Mrs. James Blue." James Blue was a pretty phony-sounding name, but the hell with it. The desk clerk didn't say anything, and the bellhop took their bags just as though they really were Mister and Mrs. James Blue from Philadelphia.

Up in the room, Vince dragged out a quarter for the bellhop. As soon as the door closed behind the bellhop, Saralee cried, "A bed!"

Eight hours sleep," Vince reminded her. "I've been driving all night."

"Oh, don't say things like that," she squealed. "It gives me goose flesh."

Vince blinked. "Say things like what?"

"That you've been driving all night. Wouldn't that be great?"

"Great," said Vince. He was beginning to suspect that Saralee Jenkins was nuts.

He managed to get undressed and crawl into the clean-sheeted double bed without anything worse from Saralee than dangerous looks. Then he said, "Wake me when I wake up," and closed his eyes.

"I'm all rested," she said. "I slept in the car. So I guess I'll go shopping."

"You do that," he said, and fell asleep at once. He didn't even hear her leave the room.

When he woke up it was twilight, and the clock on the table beside the bed said seven-thirty. He'd been racked out for more than twelve hours.

Saralee wasn't there. For an awful second, Vince was afraid she'd found somebody else already, somebody who could supply his own money and who maybe didn't need as much sleep as Vince did. Maybe she'd found that platoon.

Then he saw the note beside the clock. He picked it up and read it. It was from Saralee, and it said she was starved. He was surprised to find she hungered for other things beside sex. Anyway, it went on to say that she had gone out for something to eat, and would be back around eight o'clock.

The mention of food reminded him that he, too, was starved. It was time for that steak.

He got up, dressed, and left a note for Saralee on the back of her note. "Can't wait," the note read. "I'm hungry enough to eat the furniture. I'll be back in about an hour." He propped the note up against the clock, and turned to leave.

Then he noticed all the packages on the chairs. Saralee had said she was going shopping, and it looked as though she'd been good to her word. Vince took a second to look in the packages, saw skirts and blouses and stockings and underwear and shoes. The kid had really gone wild with her stolen loot.

Stolen loot. Better not think about that. Better to think about food.

Vince took the elevator down, then wandered around Broadway for a while, finally stopping in at a luncheonette and having a too-dry hamburger and a too-bitter cup of coffee. Then it was time to go back to the hotel room.

But he didn't feel like it, not just yet. He knew Saralee would be there now, and he knew she would be hungry again, and this time not for food. And he didn't feel quite ready for another fast round with Saralee. He wasn't up to it yet, that's all there was to it.

So he wandered around some more. He strolled down West 69th Street to Columbus Avenue, headed up Columbus, and stopped in at the first bar he saw. He ordered a beer, and the bartender didn't give him any trouble about his age, which was a relief. He sat and sipped at his beer and tried not to think things over. That wasn't too difficult, since his stomach was acting up a bit. As soon as he put some beer down, the stomach let him know there hadn't been enough food put in yet. The old hunger pains were coming back. So he'd just finish this one beer, find someplace better than the greasy spoon where he'd had the hamburger and coffee, and this time really have a meal.

It was a goofy introduction to New York. A lousy hamburger, and living on Saralee Jenkins' money. No, not Saralee Jenkins' money. Saralee Jenkins' husband's money.

That thought was enough to drive Vince from the bar.

Vince went back to Broadway, and this time found a halfway decent restaurant, where he had his steak, blood rare, and a side order of poached eggs, and a couple glasses of milk. He finished it all off with two beers. He'd had some idea of filling himself with protein, so he could go back and at least have an even chance in the coming battle with Saralee, but instead he ate too much and wound up logy and stuffed and half-asleep. So he had to go out and walk around some more, and smoke lots of cigarettes until he felt like braving the hotel.

Saralee was coming out the door of the hotel just as he was going in. They both stopped on the sidewalk, and she said, "Where've you been? I've been going frantic. I was just going looking for you."

"I was pretty hungry," he said. "I've spent all this time eating."

"It's nine o'clock, Vince," she said.

"I was pretty hungry," he repeated.

"Well," she said, twining her arm with his and leading him back inside the hotel, "you're here now, at any rate." She pressed her hip against him as they walked. "And you know what we've got upstairs, don't you?"

"No," he said. "What?"

"A real bed," she whispered.

He took a deep breath. Saralee had told him, that first time they'd been together, that once a night with a normal guy was enough for her. But apparently she'd been wrong. No wonder

Bradley Jenkins hadn't been able to keep her at home. Vince was beginning to doubt that anybody could keep Saralee Jenkins at home.

A stray ironic thought hit him. He'd started all this looking for a virgin. Instead, he'd found a nymphomaniac. How far a miss could you make?

Saralee wasn't a miss, but he could make her. He winced at that pun, and allowed Saralee to lead him into the self-service elevator.

She was a busy little girl in the elevator, all over him like a heavy fog, and when the elevator stopped at their floor, he had to readjust himself before he could step out to the hall.

The interlude in the elevator washed away all his apprehensions. As they headed down the hall for their own room, he was almost as eager as she was. It was impossible to be as eager as she.

They got into the room, and she pirouetted in delight. "A bed!" she cried, and started pulling off clothes.

Vince joined her in the disrobing act, and then he joined her in bed. "This time," she told him fiercely, "no warm-up. I'm ready to go right now. So you just come here."

"Right you are," he said.

Once was never enough for Saralee, that's all there was to it. It had to be twice.

It was eleven o'clock before she fell asleep. Vince lay there awake a little while longer, thinking about things. He had a feeling he was going to enjoy the hell out of these four days.

But he also had the feeling that he'd be ready for a vacation by the time they were through.

Chapter 6

It was a very strange vacation.

There was only one place in New York where they spent any time, and that was the hotel. And there was only one place in the hotel where they seemed to spend any time, and that was the bed. There were the mornings, and there were the afternoons, and there were the evenings. Some girls, Vince knew, had a time clock built into a very important part of their anatomy. Some could only do it properly in the morning, and others in the afternoon, and most of them at night.

Saralee wasn't the time clock type. She wasn't even the time bomb type. She was built more along the lines of a hundred-gallon drum of nitroglycerine, always ready to go off.

In the past, when Vince had gotten started in the role of a dungaree Don Juan, he had learned that you could get pretty sick of the same woman. That had happened with Rhonda. It was great, even if it did leave him feeling thoroughly conned by her mock virginity. It was great, but after a while it was the same damned thing over and over, and then all of a sudden it wasn't so great anymore.

Saralee was different. With Saralee it wasn't the same damned thing over and over. Far from it. Saralee was imaginative, and inventive, and insatiable. They had started off in the good old way, and after a while Vince had taught her a few things that he had always considered very advanced, and then she had taught him a few things that were absolutely unbelievable. If he had heard them described he would have sworn they were biologically impossible, but they weren't. Not with the two of them carrying through so successfully.

So he wasn't bored with Saralee. You couldn't be bored with Saralee, any more than you could be bored with sex in general. She just wasn't the boring sort.

Exhausting... That was more the word for it.

Vince was exhausted. He ate eggs all the time, and plenty of nearly raw meat, and drank buckets of milk, and even bolted down a dozen raw oysters once in desperation. But it didn't work. In fact, the more fit he was for horizontal games (or vertical games, depending upon Saralee's particular state of mind at the moment) the more games they played.

In fact, if he had been out of condition it would have worked out a lot better. Then he could have said that he was too tired, which he did from time to time. It didn't seem to make much difference, though. She would find something to do that would make him untired again. She found a lot of things.

And they always worked.

Some of them were things that nice girls didn't do, and some of them were things that nice girls didn't think about, and some of them were things that nice girls didn't know about. Some of them, for that matter, were things that nice whores didn't think about.

But they always worked.

By the evening of the third day Vince realized that his time limit wasn't limited enough. He'd thought that four days with Saralee wouldn't be enough. He was wrong. Four days with Saralee would be enough. Enough to kill him.

It was eight o'clock now and he was mercifully alone, eating a plateful of fried potatoes and washing them down with black coffee. Fried potatoes and black coffee did nothing at all for your virility, and this was the main reason he was eating them. What he really wanted was a blood-rare steak, but he was afraid that if he had a blood-rare steak he would find it a good deal more difficult to run out on Saralee.

Which was precisely what he was planning to do.

He stirred the coffee and took a sip of it. It was simple—Saralee was out shopping, the only other activity she found enjoyable. The stores were open until nine and she was getting in her licks. She wouldn't be back until nine-thirty at the earliest, which gave him an hour and a half at the very least.

He was in a restaurant just a block from the hotel. He would go back, get the car which Saralee had moved to the hotel's parking lot, and get the merry hell out of New York. It would be too bad about Saralee, of course, but if it was too bad about Saralee that was just too bad. He couldn't feel particularly sympathetic toward her at the moment. She was a nice kid, and she meant well, and she was sweet and good and kind, but if he didn't get away from her soon he would be dead.

Besides, Saralee would make out okay. If worse came to worse, she could always get a job. He'd heard how rough it was for an inexperienced girl to get a job in New York, but fortunately Saralee had plenty of experience in two areas. She could get a job in a drugstore behind the counter, because of all her experience in Brighton. Or she could get a job in a cathouse because of all her experience, period.

He laughed an evil laugh. It was going to be easy now. Back to the hotel. Pack the suitcase. Get the car. Drive off into the night. Stay the hell away from New York because a man could get killed if he stayed in New York long enough.

The check came to a dollar and ten cents, which was too much, but he paid it and left the waiter a forty cent tip, which was ridiculous. What the hell. It was her money, not his. He couldn't take it along, because that would be stealing. But he could tip his head off, and that would be all right.

He no longer believed old Bradley Jenkins was over forty, the way Saralee said he was, and the way he looked. It seemed that way on the surface, but after you knew Saralee the way he knew Saralee, you got a different picture.

The way he figured it, Brad Jenkins was around twenty-three. When he married Saralee, Brad was big and broad-shouldered and hungry for sex. Being married to Saralee, Vince knew, would be a pretty debilitating experience. If three days with her could demolish a guy, a year could turn him into an old man before his time. More than a year was impossible to imagine.

Poor Brad Jenkins, fainting all over the place like that. The way Vince looked at it, Brad was fainting from sheer unadulterated joy. He was fainting because he couldn't believe he'd actually managed to unload Saralee on some poor goof.

Named Vince.

The elevator deposited him on his floor and Vince walked to the room. It was simple now, very simple. He opened the door with his key, closed it behind him, and started throwing things into his suitcase. There was very little to pack and it didn't take him long.

With the suitcase closed, he went to the door again, ready to ride back down to the main floor and get his car from the garage. And just about then something profound occurred to him. It was going to be difficult, very difficult indeed, to drive that car without the key. And he didn't have the goddamned key.

Saralee had it. Saralee moved the car from the original lot to the hotel garage, and somehow in the bed-to-bed-to-bed confusion of it all, he hadn't managed to get key away from her. At the time it hadn't mattered. What the hell, he wasn't going anywhere. He didn't need car, not then. So she kept the key. It was in her purse and her purse was with her, and she was not around.

Of all the brilliant, masterful, superb displays of creative stupidity, this won the Oscar. Of all the—

He didn't unpack the suitcase. It might have been the best thing to do, so she wouldn't suspect anything, but he was willing to bet she wouldn't look in his suitcase. Not her. She would look at him, and then she would take off her clothes, and off they would go again on the old merry-go-round.

He sat down on the edge of the bed and waited. While he waited, he found a few more things to call himself and a few more things to call her. At a quarter to ten the door finally opened.

"Hi!" she called gaily. "I'm home!"

"I'm glad to see you," he said honestly.

"Miss me?"

"Uh-huh."

"Wait'll you see what I bought." She wrestled with a package, a massive white box all messed up with red ribbon. She uncovered the box triumphantly, hauling out a garment.

I mean, Vince thought, you just had to call it a garment. Because there wasn't much else you could call it. Because there wasn't much there, when you came right down to it.

It was black, and it was flimsy, and it was sheer, and it was about as concealing as a pane of glass. "What the hell is it?" he asked.

"Can't you tell?"

"Frankly, no."

"Well, what does it look like?"

"Looks like a hairnet."

She laughed. "Here," she said. "I'll model it for you. I mean, I bought it for you."

"You bought it for me?"

She nodded.

"I'd look awfully silly—"

That got another laugh. "I bought it so I could look good to you," she said. "So you can look at me while I'm wearing it and get all excited."

Here we go, he thought. Here we go, off on the goddamned merry-go-round again. She began undressing, clothes soaring all over the room, until in a short time she wasn't wearing a damned thing. Then she was wearing something, but it was the hairnet, so the effect remained about the same. The hairnet, amazingly, covered all of her from shoulders to knees. It covered all of her and concealed none of her, all at once, which was fantastic.

"Vince," she cooed, homing in on him. "Good sweet Vince. My little Vince. My baby's going to be good to me, isn't he? My baby's going to make me feel good again."

Your baby, he thought, is going to crap out completely. Your baby is going to fold up like a murphy bed. And the word bed made him wince a little. He wondered whether he'd ever be able to see a bed again without thinking of Saralee.

Or a floor, for that matter. Or a bathroom rug. Or a bathtub. Or a coat closet, or an elevator, or—

"Take off your clothes, Vince. There, Vince. Now you're as naked as I am. Nakeder, because of this thing I'm wearing. It cost thirty-five dollars, can you imagine?"

At that price it cost about three times as much, ounce for ounce, as platinum. He looked at her, and he decided that maybe the thirty-five bucks had been well spent.

"Look at me, Vince. Don't I look good? Look at my breasts. They're nice, aren't they? You know, I think they've grown since I met you. I mean, they're getting all this exercise and everything. It's stimulating them, sort of, and they're getting bigger."

If they got much bigger she'd need a suitcase to carry them in. He looked at her. She was having that old effect on him again, the effect she invariably had. He didn't want to go another round, not mentally. But his body somehow wasn't listening to his mind. His body was acting as though it had a mind of its own, which was sort of disconcerting.

He grabbed her and heaved her down on the bed. The hairnet thing fell away and he threw himself down on her, hungry for her, but now it was her turn to play. She was being coquettish. It was sort of funny, but he didn't feel like laughing.

"Not so fast," she was saying. "Let's go nice and slow now, Vince. Remember the way you teased me that day I was on fire? Remember the way you made me wait and wait and wait and I almost went out of my mind waiting so long? Now you can wait, Vince. Now you can wait until I'm good and ready."

He was being placed in the difficult position of raping a girl he didn't want in the first place. Raping a nymphomaniac, which was even worse. How in the name of the Lord did you go about raping a nymphomaniac?

And she wouldn't stop squirming around. Every time he thought he had her, she would give a little twist and laugh a mean laugh and suddenly she wasn't where she had been a second ago. It was like banging your head against a brick wall. He got hold of a breast, and held it, and felt all that creamy flesh. And then he would reach for more of her, and, suddenly, the grand prize wasn't there any more.

Saralee, he thought, you are now about to be raped. Lie back and enjoy it.

The thirty-five dollar hairnet disappeared. It was an exhilarating feeling, ripping a thirty-five dollar hairnet into gossamer wisps. It was even more exhilarating when he hauled off and belted her in the belly with his closed fist.

She let out a roar.

So he belted her again.

Then the prize was his, and it began, and suddenly he heard her bellowing like a wounded steer. Except that she didn't sound wounded at all, or, for that matter, bovine.

When it was over and he was lying on his back staring vacantly at the ceiling, he knew just what he had to do. It was the only way out, and although it might well kill him, it was the best way to get out of the hotel without her. It would not be easy, not at all, but it was the only way. He had to tell himself over and over again that it was the only way or he could never possibly go through with it. And he had to go through with it, of course, because, after all, it was the only way.

It was a simple way. Very simple.

He simply had to keep doing it to her until she passed out. Over and over again, until she couldn't take it anymore and passed out. Then he would get up and get dressed and take the car key from her purse and off he would go and the hell with her.

The second time was tough, but he did it, and when he was through he looked hopefully for signs of weariness. But she didn't look very weary. She looked ready for more.

"That was good," she told him, her eyes shining. "You know, you seem to improve with practice. You just keep getting better."

More, he thought. Got to do it again. Then she'll be so tired she'll pass out, and that will be just ginger peachy. Then I'll spring out of bed and off I'll go, back to the pea-green waters of Lake Lugubrious.

"Come on, Vince," she said. "Let's do it again. Gee I haven't had this much fun in years. For a while there, I thought you were slowing down, but I must have been wrong. Three times in a row! Gee."

Gee, he thought savagely. Gee, oh, dee, dee, ay, em, en. Gee.

The third time was sort of like trying to climb a mountain with your hands and feet tied together. The third time was sort of like swimming through sand. The third time was torture.

But the third time did the trick. He rolled away from her when it was finally over and looked down into her eyes. They had a dreamy look to them and he knew it was only a matter of seconds before she would fall asleep. Then he would bound out of bed and get that cruddy key and off he would go.

He looked at her, waiting for her to fall asleep, hoping that she would have the decency to conk out before too long. He looked at her, and he felt envious of Bradley Jenkins. Jenkins might have lost a lot of money, but now he had the chance to get his health back. Lucky Jenkins.

Her eyes closed, and her breathing leveled off, and he was ready to get up and go. He was ready, but his body wasn't ready, and he waited for a minute or two to get his strength up.

And then, abruptly, Vince passed out.

He woke up. He sat up in bed and opened his eyes. He looked over at Saralee but she wasn't there. She had managed it, had gotten up before him and vanished into New York, leaving him there.

Her purse had gone with her, which meant that his key had gone with her, which in turn meant that he was right back where he started from.

Which was nowhere. Which was up the creek in a lead canoe. Which was unpleasant.

And it had been such a perfect plan. He'd worked like a Turk, managed three masterful assaults on the castle, and then, with the prize within his grasp, he'd pulled a Bradley Jenkins. Not a faint, perhaps, but a crap-out, and it amounted to about the same thing.

His mind groped around and presented him with a marvelous mental picture. He would wait for her to return, and then they would do it again, and again, and again, and he would keep falling asleep, and he wouldn't get back to the cabin ever again. And, damn it, today was the last day he had. He couldn't afford to wait any longer.

Well, the hell with the key. He could always run a jumper wire and get the car started without it. He'd done that once before. It might look strange, might baffle the lot attendant a little, but what the hell, it was his car, and he could play games with it if he wanted to. The lot attendant's private opinion of him didn't count now. All that counted was getting back to the lake.

He pulled himself out of bed and jumped into his clothes. He picked up his suitcase, left the room and rang for the elevator. He wasn't even going to wait for breakfast, not now. He could grab a bite to eat on the road. For the time being, all he wanted was to put as much distance as possible between himself and New York.

He left the elevator, walked around to the garage and found the attendant. "I'm James Blue," he lied. "I'd like my car, please."

"Sure," the guy said. "Hang on a minute and I'll run her out for you."

The attendant disappeared and Vince steadied himself. It was suspicious, him leaving with a suitcase. Almost as though he was trying to skip out on his bill. Which, come to think of it, he was.

Well, if the attendant made any trouble, he could always leave the suitcase behind. The suitcase didn't matter. He mattered, though, and the car mattered. To hell with the suitcase.

The attendant came back smiling. "Sorry," he said. "Guess you and the missus got your signals crossed."

Vince looked blank.

"It's in the book," the attendant explained. "I wasn't on then so I didn't know, but your wife picked up the car a few minutes before eight."

Vince felt blank.

"If you don't have too far to go," the attendant said, "you can always go out front and grab a hack. Easier than driving, especially if you don't know the city. Doorman'll flag down a hack for you if you ask him."

He headed back to the room. All of a sudden he didn't feel too good.

He felt worse when he got back to the room. Much worse, because he gave the room a quick going-over and saw something, something he hadn't noticed when he jumped out of bed and headed for freedom.

The room looked the same as ever, with boxes piled all over it. But this time he looked in the boxes and made a rather startling discovery.

They were empty. Every last one of them was completely empty. So was the closet.

Which meant, pure and simple, that Saralee had decided to clear out. It wasn't enough that she had left him, but she had also made off with his car. And, undoubtedly, had also left him with the hotel bill unpaid. And no money except for the ten bucks and change he had in his wallet.

Or did he? He looked in the wallet and shuddered. The little bitch had gone through it and it was empty. Quite empty.

He was broke, and his car was gone, and the bill wasn't paid, and he had to bring the car back to his father by nightfall, and he didn't have a car to bring back, and he was broke, and he owed the damned hotel a fortune, and he had to get back to Lake Ludicrous, and...

First things first. First he had to get out of the hotel, and this time, of course, he couldn't take his suitcase with him. If he did, they might stop him. And if they stopped him there were several things they would find out. They would learn that Saralee was gone, and that all Saralee's luggage had somehow managed to accompany Saralee, and that the car was gone, and that he had been trying to get lost himself. They would also discover that he was neither James Blue nor a resident of Philadelphia, and at that point they would solve all his problems for him. They would chuck him in the tank, and they would lose the key, and that would be the end.

He left the suitcase, took the elevator to the main floor and headed for the door. He felt his hands trembling a little and hid them in his pockets.

Then he heard the voice, just behind him, saying: "Mister Blue? Could I talk to you for a minute?"

Chapter 7

Vince was never quite sure how he did it. When he turned, slowly, in answer to that ominous question, and saw facing him a bald man wearing a pinstriped suit who could have been nothing in this world but a hotel manager, his blood sank to his shoes, his heart jumped up into his throat, and he went blank. And someone else, some total stranger, using his body and his voice, snapped with obvious irritation, "What is it?"

"About this bill, Mister Blue," said the manager, holding up a squarish sheet of thin paper. "I hate to—"

"Bill?" snapped the person using Vince's body and voice. "*Bill*? When my wife walks out on me, takes my car and goes God knows where, *you* come jabbering at me about a bill?"

The manager managed to back speedily away without moving a step. "Well," he said, his face a symphony of sympathetic smiling, "well, I didn't realize—of course, I had no intention—"

"You'll get your money," the genius in Vince's body said contemptuously. "Let me worry about one thing at a time, will you?"

"Yes, of course," said the manager. He was bowing from the waist now. "Of course."

"I'll straighten things out with you," the genius in Vince said, "once I've found my goddamn wife."

"Certainly, sir," said the manager. "Of course, sir."

The genius who had control of Vince's body glared with Vince's eyes at the manager for a second longer, then spun Vince's body on Vince's heel and marched Vince the hell out of the lobby and out to the sidewalk. Then the genius went away to wherever he'd popped up from, and left Vince standing there, shaking like a leaf.

He'd gotten away with it. He'd gotten away with it! *He'd gotten away with it!*

Now, all he needed was a place to sit down for a while, until his knees could carry his weight again. Now, all he needed was a place to sit down and a strong black cup of coffee and a dime to pay for the coffee. And his father's car back, so he could go home again. And Saralee standing in front of him, so he could beat her lovely face in.

It was so clear now, so goddam clear. She'd gotten up—it must have been seven o'clock or earlier, since the garage attendant said she took off with the car at eight—she'd gotten up, and she'd noticed Vince's suitcase all packed and ready to go. And she had realized that Vince was on the verge of taking a fast powder. So she had decided that she would take that fast powder herself, before little Vince had the chance.

It was now just about noon. She had a four-hour start on him. She also had money, and he didn't, not a dime. She also had a means of transportation, and he didn't, not a pogo stick.

What Vince had been doing to her physically all week, she had just done to him figuratively. And she'd been a lot better at it than him. When *she* did it, she was thorough. There wasn't any need for seconds.

Coffee. He needed coffee, and a place to sit down and try to think. That was the first thing. He couldn't just stand here, on the sidewalk in front of the hotel, until that manager in there had a chance to think things over and decide maybe Mister James Blue ought to hang around the hotel awhile and wait for his erring wife where the manager could keep an eye on him.

As if in answer to his thoughts about coffee, a bum picked that minute to panhandle him. He was a short, scrawny, scrubby little bum, with a short, scrawny, scrubby little beard. He came staggering up, dressed like a picture on a CARE poster, with a pathetic expression on his rummy face and his filthy hand held out, palm up, and he whined, "You got a dime for a cup of coffee, Mister?"

Vince just looked at him. He opened his mouth, and closed it, and opened it again, and closed it again, and finally said, in a calm and reasonable voice, "If I had a dime for a cup of coffee, you stupid son-of-a-bitch, I would *drink* a cup of coffee."

The bum blinked, and looked aggrieved. "Jeez," he whined. "You don't have to get that way about it." And he went staggering off to panhandle somebody else.

Vince took off in the opposite direction. It was too dangerous to hang around in front of the hotel any longer.

He'd walked two blocks, trying to think about what to do about Saralee and the car but managing only to think about the fact that what he needed now was a cup of coffee and a place to sit down and think things out, when he suddenly had a brilliant idea.

He stepped into the next doorway he saw. He took off his tie and slipped it into his coat pocket. Then he turned his coat collar up, unbuttoned his white shirt halfway down and pulled one shirt tail out so it dangled down below the bottom of the suit coat. He rubbed his hands on the sidewalk until they were good and sooty, then rubbed them on his face until *it* was good and sooty. Then he stepped back out among the pedestrians and looked for a likely prospect.

One came along almost immediately. A youngish guy in his mid-twenties, walking arm in arm with his girl. Vince figured a guy with a girl would be afraid to look cheap in her eyes, and so would be an easy touch. He stepped in front of the couple, a pathetic expression on his face and his now-filthy hand extended palm upward, and whined, "You got a dime for a cup of coffee, Mister?"

The victim looked embarrassed. He stopped and fidgeted for a second, and mumbled something, while the girl with him looked curiously at Vince, and then he stuck his hand into his pocket and came out with a handful of change. "Here," he mumbled, and dropped half a buck into Vince's waiting palm. Then he hurried on by.

Not only a cup of coffee. A cup of coffee and a hamburger. With onions.

Sitting in the luncheonette, dawdling over his coffee and hamburger, Vince thought it out.

Saralee was gone. So was the car. They were together, Saralee and the car.

Vince needed the car. He was supposed to go back to the lake today, so his father could drive the car home and get back to work when his vacation ended.

Vince wanted to kick the crap out of Saralee while wearing hobnail boots and brass knuckles.

Vince had to have the car, and he wanted to get his hands on Saralee. And since the car and Saralee were together, once he had found one of them, he would have both of them.

That brought up the first question. Where would Saralee have gone? Where would an ambitious, unscrupulous, good-looking nymphomaniac with a stolen car and about three hundred stolen dollars go?

She wouldn't go east because there was nothing east of New York but New England, and New England was kind of famous for prudery, and a girl like Saralee wouldn't even think of going to an area that was famous, rightly or wrongly, for prudery. And she wouldn't go north, because there was nothing to the north but lots of New York State, and then the Canadian border, and she'd never get over the Canadian border in a stolen car for which she didn't have any registration.

Come to think of it, Saralee didn't even have a license. He remembered her telling him that, after she had driven the car from the parking lot to the hotel, and how relieved he'd been that she hadn't been involved in any of the thousand minor accidents that happened every day in midtown Manhattan.

Getting back to the geography, she wouldn't head west because that way lay Brighton. The only direction left was south. Okay, she would go south. Now what?

He turned it around and looked at it from another point of view. Where would a girl like Saralee fit in? Where would a girl like Saralee naturally gravitate for?

Only two places: California and Miami.

There were lots of things against California. In the first place, it was three thousand miles away. And Saralee only had about three hundred bucks left out of the five hundred she'd lifted from Bradley Jenkins. You don't take a car three thousand miles on three hundred bucks. Not if you plan to do any eating yourself.

In the second place, in order to get to California she would first have to drive toward Brighton.

In the third place, Miami was to the south, which is the direction she would naturally take anyway.

In the fourth place, Miami was only one thousand miles away, which a girl could do on three hundred dollars.

Okay, that answered question number one. Saralee, without a shred of doubt, was headed for Miami. Now for question number two.

Question two: How the hell was Vince going to get to Miami? Once he was there, how the hell was he going to find one sharp broad in a town full of sharp broads?

He sat there for a long while, and he just didn't get any answers to question number two. The coffee got cold, and the hamburger got colder, and the hamburger bun got hard, and he still didn't have any answers to question number two. The waitress began to glare at him and he still didn't have any answers to question number two.

He finally left the place, noticing that it was now one o'clock, and Saralee now had a five-hour start on him.

Saralee didn't have a driver's license and she was driving a stolen car. Therefore, Saralee was going to be obeying every speed law she came across. Which meant it would take her two days at the very least to get to Miami, and probably three. The first day, she would maybe be able to drive four or five hundred miles.

Then she'd clock out at a motel somewhere, and start off bright and early tomorrow morning.

If Vince had a car, he'd be able to at least catch up with her. He could drive all night, if need be, and finally he'd catch up with her, because she'd be obeying the speed limits, and she'd be stopping for sleep.

But Vince didn't have a car.

And he didn't have lots of time either. He was supposed to be back at the lake today. He might be able to get away with overshooting for a day, coming back tomorrow, but it just wasn't possible to never go back there, or to go back without his father's car.

He wandered around and occasionally, when he saw a likely customer, he panhandled a bit, because he at least needed eating money, and within half an hour he had three bucks. Which was a pretty good wage, averaging out to six dollars an hour.

He could always stay in New York, of course. Stay here forever, panhandling at six bucks an hour. Because he definitely could not go back to the lake without his father's car. He definitely could not, and that was all there was to it.

He saw a gas station, one of the cramped little hole-in-the-wall gas stations common to Manhattan, and stopped in, on impulse, to get some road maps. There wasn't any one road map for all of the Eastern Seaboard, but he got a bunch of state maps, and could go from one to the next, and follow Saralee's route from New York to Miami. Then he went down to 72nd Street and Broadway, where they had benches on the mall, and sat down to look at the maps.

The thing was, there were so many roads. You had your choice of half a dozen roads going out of New York, and about half a dozen roads the rest of the way.

But Saralee would be in a hurry. She would take the shortest, straightest route. Vince searched his pockets for a pencil, found one, and marked out on the maps what he thought would probably be her route. He worked at it slowly and carefully, and by the time was finished, he was ninety-nine percent sure he knew every inch of road Saralee would be traveling.

It was two o'clock. Saralee was six hours ahead of him.

He looked at his maps, and he swore under his breath, and he felt horribly frustrated. And all at once, he got his idea.

It wasn't a very good idea, but that didn't matter. That didn't matter, because it was the only idea. It was his only chance. He was sure of his reasoning all the way, sure that Saralee would be heading for Miami, almost dead sure he had figured out her complete route. If his reasoning was correct, his idea just might work. If his reasoning wasn't correct, his idea didn't matter and it didn't matter what he did, because Saralee and the car and everything else were gone forever anyway.

So the idea was worth trying, even though it wasn't very good.

He got to his feet and crossed the street to the subway station. He paid fifteen cents of his panhandled money and took the subway downtown. He made a couple of transfers, paid another quarter, and wound up on the H&M tubes, headed for Jersey. While in that last train, he put his tie back on, buttoned his shirt, turned his coat collar back down, and tucked his shirt-tail in. When the train reached the last stop in Jersey, everybody got off, and Vince was alone in the car for a minute. He pulled one of the advertising posters down from the row above the windows, hid it under his coat, and left the station.

The Delaware, Lackawanna and Western railroad station was right next to the last H&M tube stop. Vince went over there and stopped off in the men's room. There he washed the panhandling dirt from his face and hands, and carefully wrote UNIVERSITY OF MIAMI on the back of the poster in large, thick, letters. Then he went out to the waiting room, found a likely-looking untended suitcase, picked it up, and left the depot. He spent a dollar and a quarter on a cab to take him to the highway, and then he stood beside the road, the stolen suitcase next to his feet, the sign in his left hand, and his right hand out, thumb extended.

He waited five minutes before a new DeSoto screeched to a halt. He picked up the suitcase, ran to the car, and the driver, a thirtyish salesman type with horn-rimmed glasses, said, "I'm only going as far as Baltimore."

"That's fine," Vince told him. "Every little bit counts."

He tossed his suitcase into the backseat, slid into the front seat beside the driver, and said it again, his eyes staring down the road, southward. "Every little bit counts."

A truck took him from Baltimore to Washington. He didn't get to see much of the country, because he slept most of the way. He knew he was going to have to be wide-awake later on, so he forced himself to relax and sleep while he could.

Actually, it wasn't that tough to get to sleep. He'd had a very active four days, coupled with some nervous running around today, and whizzing along a superhighway on a sunny summer afternoon was pretty relaxing anyway. He conked out within ten minutes in the salesman's car, and didn't wake up till they reached Baltimore. Then the salesman wished him luck, Vince thanked the guy for the ride, closed the door, stuck out his thumb, and a truck stopped. Just like that. He was running in luck, and he hoped it kept up that way.

By the time he got to Washington, he was pretty hopeful. The salesman had driven like a madman, and the truck driver hadn't been any slouch either. Both of them had gone a hell of a lot faster than Saralee would dare to, and Vince figured by now he couldn't be more than four hours behind her.

Then came Washington, and things slowed down to a crawl. For one thing, the truck driver let him off at the northern edge of the city, which meant he was going to have to work his way all the way through Washington, and he knew from experience that hitchhiking within a city is hell. For another thing, he was beginning to feel starved, and the money he could have spent on a fast cab-ride through town had to go for food. And the eating of the food took time, too, no matter how fast he tried to chew.

Then he was back on the street again, thumbing once more. And, as he'd expected, hitchhiking through the city was hell. He did it in four short rides, with long waits in between. And the fourth ride didn't turn out to be so short after all.

It was a woman, driving a new Pontiac convertible, the incredibly expensive car for people with enough money to buy a Cadillac convertible and not enough sense to come in out of the rain.

This woman was about forty. He didn't know whether she had any sense or not, but she very obviously had money. She was dressed in an obviously expensive blue suit and, even though it was warm as hell in Washington, a waist-length fur jacket over it. On her head was one of those goofy hats that was one-tenth hat and nine-tenths veil. She was a good-looking woman for forty, as far as the face was concerned. The fur made it impossible to tell much about the body, though her nylon-sheathed legs looked pretty good from the knee down.

She stopped the car next to him, smiled, and said, "Hop in."

"Thank you, ma'am," he said, and hopped in. He'd barely had his thumb out, not expecting a woman to stop for a hitchhiker, and the fact that she had stopped surprised him so much it took him a second or two to react.

Once his suitcase and University of Miami sign were stowed in back, and he was seated in front beside the woman, the Pontiac slid away from the curb and purred southward through the evening traffic.

After a minute, the woman said, "I went to Miami, too. Quite a number of years ago."

Vince tensed. He knew what was coming next, a lot of talk about the new buildings and the old professors and how the old town is getting on and all that garbage, none of which Vince would be able to handle, since he'd never been near either Miami or its university in his life. "Well, uh," he said. "Uh, as a matter of fact I don't go there myself. My brother does. I'm going down to visit him. This'll be my first trip down there." There, he thought, that ought to do it.

The woman turned to look at him for a second, smiled and said, "Crap." Then she looked back at the street.

Vince blinked. He gaped at the woman, and waited for her to explain what that had been all about, but apparently she had no intention of doing so. She just kept driving along, a half-smile on her lips. He noticed that they were good lips, just slightly touched with lipstick, and that her hair was in a tight permanent that wasn't blowing around even though the convertible's top was down. Black hair it was, with just a touch of gray in some of the hairs at the side. It looked good on her, very sophisticated. She looked like a real heller who had grown older gracefully.

They drove two blocks in silence, and then the woman said, "Well? Aren't you going to defend yourself?"

Vince decided the only thing to do was let this graying chick have the lead, until he could figure out where she thought she was going. "Defend myself?" he asked. "From what?"

"You don't have any brother in the University of Miami," she said. She glanced over at him, smiled again, and looked back at the traffic. "That sign of yours is just something to make it easier for you to get a ride."

Vince shrugged. This time, he thought, the best thing to do was admit everything and say nothing. "It's pretty tough to get a ride," he said, "unless you do something like that."

The woman nodded. "I know it is," she said. "You're absolutely right." She glanced at him again, looked back at the road, and said, "What's that bulge inside your coat? Is that a gun?"

"Gun?" Vince hadn't even known he had a bulge inside his coat. He looked down, and realized all the road maps tucked into his inside coat pocket did make a healthy bulge. Now that he thought about it, with a bulge like that in his coat, it was a miracle he'd gotten any rides at all. And here this was the sixth person to pick him up. And this one was even a woman.

"Well?" she asked him. "Is it a gun?"

"No," he said. He grinned uneasily, not sure what this crazy woman was leading up to. "Heck, no," he said, playing it boyish. "Nothing like that. It's just road maps. See?" He dragged them out of his pocket and showed them to her. "I really am going to Miami," he said. "And I've got these road maps so I won't get lost."

The woman looked at the road maps, looked at him, stopped smiling, looked out at the street again, and said, "How disappointing."

A nut, decided Vince. That's what she was, a grade A, first-prize, number one nut.

He didn't know just how nutty she was. They were in the southern part of the city now, near the Potomac, and Vince was surprised to see that they were coming to wooded sections among the built-up areas. And he had the crazy feeling they were going the wrong way.

The feeling got stronger, a lot stronger, when the woman suddenly made a turn onto an unpaved street and drove down past two rows of unfinished ranch-style houses to the end, and stopped.

Vince looked around, half-expecting a couple of guys to come running out of one of the half-built houses and grab him. "What's going on?" he demanded. "What is this?"

"You're an awful disappointment," the woman said. She was sitting half-turned in the seat, facing him, and she was half-smiling again, her eyes shining at him in the moonlit darkness. "I certainly didn't expect anything like this when I picked you up," she said. "You turned out to be a complete flop, do you know that?"

"Well, for God's sake," Vince cried, "what the hell do you want from me?"

"Isn't that obvious?" she asked him. "I want you to rape me."

He could only stare at her. He couldn't say a word or do a thing or move a muscle, all he could do was just sit there in the car in the moonlight and stare at her.

"If you look over that way," she said, pointing beyond him, "you'll see lights. There are lots of houses all around here full of people. If you don't rape me, I'll throw you out of the car, and then I'll tear my clothes and go to one of those houses and say you *did* rape me. And I don't suppose it would take the police very long to find you. You'd be on foot, and you don't know Washington at all."

A nut, thought Vince for the thousandth time. A complete and utter nut.

The woman watched him, growing impatient. "Well?" she demanded.

"Well—" said Vince. He was trying to think. This nut wanted to be raped, that's all. That's why she'd picked him up, because she heard women who picked up hitchhikers got raped, and she got it into her head she'd liked to get raped herself.

So, what the hell, how long could it take? And it might even be fun.

But then a sudden thought struck him. "How do I know," he asked her, "that you won't call the cops afterward, anyway?"

"I won't," she said. "I promise you I won't."

"Yeah, sure, but how do I know?"

"You *know*," she reminded him, "that I *will* call the police if you *don't* rape me."

He thought that one over for a minute. It looked as though he didn't have much choice. "Okay," he said, and reached for her.

She slapped his hand away. "I didn't say make me," she said. "I said rape me. You're going to have to work for it." And she pushed the door open on her side and scampered out of the car.

She didn't run very fast. In the first place, she was wearing one of those tight hobble skirts it was impossible to walk in, much less run. And in the second place, she wasn't trying very hard.

Vince caught her after six steps. They were on ground that was going to be somebody's front lawn some day, but was now just churned-up dry earth. Vince caught the woman by one shoulder, twisted her around, and she lost her balance and fell heavily onto the ground. He dropped to his knees beside her and grabbed.

"Don't rip my clothes!" she cried, in a shrill half-whisper. "Don't rip them!"

Vince looked at her, her straining face staring up at him, and he knew this woman wanted to be roughed up. And he was willing to go along with that. All he had to do was think about the fact that she was delaying him, and that she had threatened him with the law. And all he had to do was make believe she was Saralee Jenkins. That's all he had to do, and then he could rough her up to her heart's content. And then some.

So he belted her open-handed across the face, and snapped, "If you don't want them ripped, pull them off. And do it fast."

"Yes. Yes." She struggled, lying on the ground next to him, pulling her skirt up and her panties off, and he saw that she had surprisingly good legs, that she was a woman who had cared for her body all of her life, and it had responded by staying firm and shapely long after most women were well into the sag-stage.

He slapped her again and said, "Get that fur thing off too."

She did. She was panting and moaning and half-crying, staring up at him with a crazy combination of terror and desire on her face, and she struggled around until she got the fur piece and the jacket and blouse off, and then he reached down, inserted his fingers under her bra between the breasts, and yanked upward, ripping the bra in two. The bra fell away on both sides, and he slapped her hard, forehand and backhand.

She moaned and rolled over, trying to crawl away. He smacked her naked buttocks, grabbed her hip with pinching fingers and digging nails, and pulled her back around and down again. He had his own clothes open, and he was ready, and he fell on her.

She lashed at him, screaming through clenched teeth, trying to buck him off her, but he held on grimly. All the workouts he'd had with Saralee had made it possible for him to last a long time, and he was glad of it. He wanted the time, he wanted to give this woman all she wanted and then some, he wanted to make her sorry she'd ever threatened him, sorry she'd ever come out looking for this tonight. His hands slapped and pinched and pummeled her body, until finally she opened her mouth in a full-throated scream, and her fighting changed, became more real, and she shrieked, "Stop! Stop! Stop!"

But he couldn't stop, and he wouldn't stop. And now she wasn't fighting him, either make-believe or real, now she was blending with him.

Slowly, his breath came back, slowly his awareness, of the place and the circumstances came back, and slowly he crawled off her and got shakily to his feet, readjusting his clothes. And the woman lay on her back, her skirt a wrinkled mess around her waist, her jacket and blouse and panties lying dirt-stained around her, and she smiled up at him, sighing, and whispered, "You weren't such a disappointment, after all. Once you got started, you weren't a disappointment at all."

Now, he was sick of her. He felt used, cheapened, as he had never felt with a girl before. This woman had dragged him down into her own sickness and made him a part of it. He remembered how he had slapped her and clawed her, and how he had enjoyed doing it, and he felt sick and ashamed, and wanted nothing but to get away from here.

She got slowly to her feet, straightening her skirt as best she could, donning again her blouse and jacket and fur. Balling up her panties and ripped bra, she said, "Come on. I'll drive you across the Potomac."

He thought of saying no, but then he remembered how important time was, that he had to make up for a lot of lost time, and so he nodded and walked back to the car with her. There, she put the panties and bra on the floor in back and slid in behind the wheel, as Vince got in on the other side. All at once, he noticed that she was still wearing that nine-tenths veil hat, that she'd worn it all the way through the fake rape-scene. And for some reason, that struck him as the sickest part of it all, that she'd worn that stupid little Sunday-tea hat all during the phony rape scene.

She drove him out of Washington, then across the Potomac and through Alexandria to a good spot for him to hitchhike from. As he was getting out of the car, she leaned toward him, her hand held out, and said, "Thanks. You did a good job."

He had the suitcase and sign in his left hand. He reached out the right hand, she dropped something into it, and her car spun around and headed back for Washington. Puzzled, Vince looked at what she had given him. A roll of bills. Ten tens. One hundred dollars.

He got another truck ride out of Alexandria, and this time he was really in luck. The guy was going all the way to Miami. Vince was about six hours behind by now and he was glad he wasn't going to be losing any more time between rides.

This guy was driving an overload of tile pipe, so he didn't exceed any speed limits. Vince was just as well pleased. He was coming into the territory where he was going to be very interested in the roadside scenery, particularly around the motels, so he was glad the truck wasn't going to be whipping by too fast to see anything.

What he was looking for was his father's Packard. He was glad, for one of the few times in his life, that it was a Packard. There were damn few of them on the road anymore, particularly dull gray ones. He wouldn't be likely to miss it.

They headed on down across Virginia and into North Carolina, following the route Vince had marked out on the roadmaps back in New York, and every time they passed a motel, Vince took careful inventory of the cars parked in front.

He struck pay dirt just south of Charlotte, almost into South Carolina. A dull-gray Packard, right year, what looked like the right license plates in the dim motel light. She'd gotten pretty far in one day.

"Stop here," Vince told the driver. "I get out here."

"I thought you were going to Miami."

"I just saw my roommate's car back at that motel. He can take me the rest of the way."

The truck driver was plainly puzzled, but he stopped the car. "Anything you say, buddy," he said.

"Thanks a lot for the lift," Vince told him. "I really appreciate it."

Then the truck was gone, and Vince was walking back toward the motel. He threw the sign and suitcase away. He wouldn't be needing those anymore.

He went up to the motel, noticing that the office was dark, which wasn't surprising. It was almost four in the morning. He walked on down the row of motel units to the one with the Packard in front, and tried the door. It was locked, which didn't faze him. He took one step back, took careful aim, raised one foot, and kicked the doorknob a good one.

As he'd supposed, the lock was pretty flimsy. The door flew open, and he walked on in. The light switch was beside the door. He flicked it on, closed the door behind him, and grinned at the wide-eyed girl sitting up in the bed.

"Hello, Saralee," he said. "Surprised to see me?"

Chapter 8

The kid was awfully nervous. He was about Vince's age but looked a lot younger. His face was round and rosy like a highly polished apple. His eyes were the kind that were scared to look back when you looked at them. It was a shame, Vince thought, that you had to deal with people like this. But money was money. You couldn't be too choosy, not when money was money and you needed it in a hurry.

"Hot as a pistol," Vince went on, coaxing the boy, leading him gently by the nose. "Built like a bomb shelter. Young, too. Good stuff. You won't regret it, believe me. Money well spent and all that. You know."

"Gee," the kid said. "I mean . . . gee."

"And she'll do anything," said Vince, giving the kid a sly man-of-the-world grin. "Anything you want. Anything at all."

"Anything?"

"Anything," Vince emphasized. He would have sworn the stupid bastard's mouth was beginning to water.

"Well," said the kid. "I mean, twenty bucks is a lot of money. You can't just reach out your hand and there's twenty bucks."

Vince reminded him that the motel where the kid was staying with his folks cost more than that for a day. Then he went into another profound description of Saralee's assets. That did it.

"I'll get the money," the kid said. "Hang on."

Vince stood there with his face hanging out while the kid went to get the money. *Maybe he'll steal it from his old man,* he thought. *Or maybe he'll just tell the old man Hey, gimme twenty bucks so I can get laid, and the old man'll come across with the twenty.*

It was a pretty horrible thought.

"I got it," the kid said, returning. "Let's get going. I mean, we might as well get it over with, don't you think? I mean, there's no point in wasting any time."

Vince didn't feel like talking anymore. He pointed at the Packard and the kid got in. Vince slipped behind the wheel, played games with the ignition, leaned on the accelerator and aimed the car at Saralee's motel. The kid would be tossing another twenty bucks in the sack, and Saralee would be tossing another kid in the sack, and this should be cause for rejoicing. Somehow it wasn't. Somehow he felt pretty cruddy.

It was, he reflected, damned hard work being a pimp.

Vince was standing outside the door, smoking a cigarette and listening to Saralee showing the kid what it was all about. If anybody had told him he'd be pimping in North Carolina, he would have laughed. But here he was, pimping in North Carolina. And what the hell was so funny?

When he broke in on Saralee, first she tried to explain, and then she tried to apologize, and finally she tried to seduce him. But this time her attempts at seduction were as ineffectual as her apologies and her explanations. Maybe he was growing immune to Saralee or something. Whatever it was, her body did nothing to change his mind.

At first he had wanted to beat the living crap out of her, but the phony rape bit with the tired old broad in Washington had taken it out of his system. He just didn't feel up to slapping another woman. Some guys got their kicks that way, but he didn't seem to be one of them. Besides, he'd come a long way. You don't hitchhike all the way from New York to North Carolina just to knock some girl's head in.

And there were more important considerations. The most important consideration was getting the car back to his old man, and this turned out to be impossible. Saralee wasn't much of a driver. The Packard was a wreck to begin with, but she hadn't bothered to put any oil into it. The poor heap knocked and rattled and huffed and puffed. It wouldn't make Baltimore, much less New York. And if he gave the car back to his old man in that shape, he might as well hang himself.

That's where the money came in. With enough money, he could fly back to New York and take a bus to the lake. His father would be annoyed, but he'd get back soon enough so that the old man wouldn't exactly hit the roof. Then, with enough money, he could pay his father for the car. Make up some story about how it got wrecked, and hand his father a mittful of money. That might do the trick.

The problem, then, was money. He had the hundred bills from the Rape-Me Relic, and Saralee, he found out quickly, had almost three hundred of her own.

Which wasn't enough.

It would cost him, say, a hundred dollars to get back to the lake. The car might bring a hot fifty bucks on the open market now, but his father would expect at least five hundred for it. And he didn't dare sell the car.

The thing was, he and Saralee had a little less than four hundred between them. And he needed a bare minimum of six hundred—one hundred to get back to the lake and five hundred to pay for the car. Seven hundred would be more like it, and eight hundred would be fine, but six hundred would do in a pinch.

And if this wasn't a pinch, nothing was.

The answer had been simple. Saralee would hustle for the money. She would stay in the room, and he would scout likely prospects and bring them to the room where she would accommodate them. He told Saralee about it, and she was against it, claiming that she would give it away to anybody but the idea of selling it repelled her.

"It's the same as giving it away," he told her. "Because I'll be taking all the money. You won't get a nickel of it."

This didn't placate her. But pretty soon she managed to see that she didn't have a hell of a lot of choice in the matter. First of all, he took all of her clothes and put them in the trunk of the car. That left her naked, and restricted her movements to the immediate vicinity of the room itself. Then he told her precisely what she would look like after he got through with her if she didn't do as expected. She shuddered a little.

Getting customers could have been easier, but it also could have been harder. Vince knew the type to work on. Kids his age, rich kids on vacation. Nice virginal type kids who wouldn't make any trouble and who would pay plenty for a chance to be with

Saralee. The South seemed to swarm with kids like that. They were all over the place.

The door opened and the kid walked out. He had a stupid grin all over his polished apple face. "Everything okay?" Vince asked him. "You get what you paid for?"

The kid nodded, still grinning, and headed off down the road. It was a good mile to the motel where he was staying and Vince started to offer him a ride. Then he decided the kid was so high on Saralee he could probably *fly* back.

Vince walked into the room, closing the door behind him. "That's six of them," he told her. "How's it going? How's the old machinery holding up?"

He expected her to be a little bitter, but she wasn't. She smiled dreamily, running her hot hands over her hot body and purring like a kitten.

"Wonderful," she said. "Just wonderful. I never had so many boys at once before. One after the other. It's wonderful."

"Well," Vince said. "Well, a few more and we can call it quits. We've got over five hundred now. As soon as we hit six, you can take it easy."

"I am taking it easy," she insisted. "This is fun. Hurry up and get some more, will you?"

"You're insatiable."

"What's that mean?"

"It means you never get enough."

She licked her lips. "You hurry up and get some more," she said, "or I'll rape you."

He shook his head, then walked out and got in the car. The next motel he came to was like striking gold. There were six of them there, six kids seventeen and eighteen years old, and all of them were about as interested in Saralee as it was possible for a person to be. They were ready to go, and they didn't haggle over the price, and that meant a very fast hundred and twenty dollars, which was enough to retire on. He loaded them into the Packard and stepped on the gas.

On the way the boys kept talking about what they were going to do. They had some fairly unusual ideas. They weren't going to stand around waiting in line, not them. They wanted sort of a party with all of them in there at once. Vince felt like telling them they were sick, but he had decided that pimping was one of those occupations where the customer was always right.

But he did have a good money idea.

"Look," he said, "something like you got in mind, you got to have what is known as a package deal. That's what we call it in the trade. A package deal."

He sounded so professional that he scared himself. But right away they asked him what he meant by a package deal.

"Well," he said, "the twenty dollar price, that's for one man. You understand? But if you want sort of a party, then the price arrangement is different. What it is, you pay a lump sum by the hour. Then you can do whatever you want, all of you, as much as you want. It's like you were renting the girl for the hour."

He left it dangling there, waiting for them to bite, and they bit. They asked how much it was by the hour, and he told them it was a hundred dollars an hour, with a two-hour minimum. That way they wouldn't have to worry about how many times, or what they were doing, or anything. They would pay him the two hundred dollars and do whatever they wanted.

They went for it. They got all excited, as a matter of fact, and before long he was standing in front of the door again, counting the money and waiting for the two hours to pass. He didn't want to wait for two hours, not really. He didn't want to stand outside the door while all that nonsense was going on inside the door, either, and it suddenly occurred to him that there was no reason in the world for him to stick around. He had the money, and he didn't give a hydroelectric dam what happened to Saralee.

So why stay around?

He hopped into the car again, and drove to the Charlotte Airport. There was a flight to Idlewild leaving in half an hour, and because of a last-minute cancellation there was a seat open, and he took it. He got on the plane and studied the pretty breasts of the stewardess, which made him think once more of Saralee.

Poor Saralee. He'd played a dirty trick on her, all things considered. A hell of a dirty trick. She didn't have a dime, and she didn't have a car—not with the Packard parked at the airport. And, he realized all at once, she didn't have a goddamned thing to wear. All her clothing was stashed in the trunk of the Packard. He'd put it there to keep her from running out, and now it looked as though she was going to do very little running out indeed. He tried to feel sorry for her, but it seemed as though every time he tried to feel really sympathetic towards her, he burst into uncontrollable laughter.

Poor Saralee, he would think. Then Ha-ha-ha-ha-ha. And so on, with all the other passengers staring at this idiot who kept breaking up and laughing all over the place. Let 'em stare, he thought. Hell with them.

He settled back finally, and relaxed in his chair, and, because he was very tired, fell asleep. He woke up as the plane was bouncing through some air pockets. His ears were popping and his head ached dully. Then the pilot set the plane on the ground and everything was all right again.

He took a bus to the East Side Terminal, and a cab to the Port Authority bus terminal, and another bus that made fifteen stops, the last of which was Lake Ludicrous. And then, finally, he was at the lake, and then at the cabin, and there was his father.

"You're late," his father said, "and the car's gone, and what the hell happened to you?"

Vince took a deep breath. "The car," he began. "Some idiot came down the wrong way on a one-way street and hit the car. Knocked it for a loop."

His father stared.

"I was lucky I wasn't killed," Vince added, which was true in a way. "But don't worry about the car. The guy paid for it."

"Paid for it?"

"He wasn't insured," Vince said. "I could have sued him down the river, and he was all shook up, so he offered to pay for it. I've got the money. I figured suing him would just take a lot of time and get him into all kinds of trouble. He was a pretty nice guy, too. Stupid, and a hell of a driver, but a nice guy."

"How much?"

"Huh?"

"For the car," his father said. "How much did you get for it?"

"Oh," Vince said. "Well, six hundred dollars."

His father stared. "You're kidding," he said. "You have to be kidding. You can't mean it."

"It wasn't enough?"

Softly, his father said: "Perhaps, on a good day, I could have sold the car for a hundred and fifty dollars. On a bad day, maybe half of that. And you—" he said reverently, "—got six hundred beautiful round dollars for it."

Vince took the money from his pocket. "The guy was scared," he elaborated, "and he just wanted to get rid of me, I guess. Here's the money."

His father counted the money, his eyes shining happily. "Vince," he said. "Good old Vince. My son. Chip off the old block. Only kid in creation who could make a pile of dough by cracking up a car. You're a good boy, Vince. Any car I ever have, you be sure and borrow it. Borrow all of 'em. Great boy, Vince."

"Gee," Vince said. This was going much better than he had expected.

"Vince, I can't keep all of this. You were the one who swung the deal. You ought to get sort of a commission. You know—a piece of the profit."

His father was pushing money at him, telling him go out and have himself a big time. Vince walked away shaken, and looked at the money in his hand. He counted it, after awhile, and discovered that there was a hundred and fifty bucks there. Which was quite a bit of money. Even with inflation, and all that, and the shrinking dollar, and the high cost of living, even with all those things to take into consideration, one hundred and fifty bucks was a lot of money.

So here we are, he thought. Back at old Lake Lollapalooza, with a fistful of dough and no place to go. Now just where in hell do we go from here?

• • •

The first place he went was to take a shower, because he stank a little, and to change his clothes, because they stank a lot. Then he went down to the lake and slept in the sunshine, which was fun, sort of. Then, because he was hungry, he went and had something to eat. After lunch he went back to the lake, on the prowl again for female flesh. There were plenty of likely-looking prospects, but somehow he couldn't get interested. He would look at the girls and imagine what they would look like without any clothes on. Then he would imagine how they would be in the hay, and he would decide that it probably wouldn't be much fun at all.

He was frightened. Maybe he was losing his interest in sex. Maybe he had burned himself out, or something, and he couldn't get excited by a woman again.

That didn't seem too likely. But there was something he found out that day, and it became more apparent during the next week. They spent part of the next week there at the lake, and then his father picked up a second-hand car at a good price and they drove back to Modnoc. At Modnoc it became obvious. The domestic life just wasn't exciting enough. Modnoc and the lake, both at once, were totally lacking in points of interest. He was bored stiff.

Well, he told himself, it was no wonder. In the past month or so he'd done one hell of a boatload of fascinating things. He had had two virgins who weren't virgins, and then he had put the blocks to a married woman, and then the married woman turned out to be a nymphomaniac. Then he and the married woman ran off to New York, with the married woman's husband's hard-earned cash, and registered in a hotel and played sex marathon.

Then the gal left him, and he begged on street corners, and skipped a hotel bill, and hitchhiked to Carolina, and raped a girl on command, and found the married woman, and made her whore for him, and left her naked and penniless, and flew back to New York, and here he was.

Which was a lot of activity. And which made Modnoc seem more than ever a tasteless, lifeless, useless place to spend his life.

He thought what it would be like to spend his life in Modnoc. He would go back to school in the fall, graduate the following June, and then go to college. Four dull years at a dull college and he would be back, taking a "good job" with the Modnoc Plastics company, marrying some stupid virgin or near-virgin, raising a batch of grubby kids and playing the good old American game.

For three days in Modnoc he lay around the house waiting for time to pass. He thought about how nice it would be to leave Modnoc, to go somewhere else on his own. Hell, it wasn't hard to be on your own. He'd managed well enough there with Saralee. She had conned him, of course, but then he turned around and conned her right back and came out of it smelling like a rose. If he left Modnoc now he would not have a car to worry about, and he would not have to come back at any set time. He could work things whatever way he wanted to work things. He would have all the room he needed to move around in. It would be a pleasure. He would go wherever he wanted, and he would do whatever he wanted, and if anybody didn't like it, to hell with them.

It sounded good. But he spent his time thinking about it rather than doing anything about it. The days dragged by until he couldn't stand it any longer. So Friday night he finally went out of the house, anxious to find something to do.

He found Sheila Kirk, who was slightly better than nothing.

Sheila Kirk had always been around, and Vince had been convinced that she had always been available. There were no stories about her one way or the other, but she had that "Available" look in her eyes. For some reason, he had never taken her up on it. It didn't make any sense, really, because she was one hell of a good-looking girl.

One *hell* of a good-looking girl. Soft brown hair and very pale skin and a pretty face and good legs and an almost unbelievable pair of mammaries. She was good-looking, and she was available, and somehow he had never answered the door when this particular opportunity had come knocking.

Well, that would have to change.

He spotted her on the street, and he walked over to her, and he said hello, and she said hello, and from there it went according to formula. She told him how lucky he was to get to the lake because Modnoc was dead as a doornail in the summer, and he told her it couldn't be that dead if she was around, and they went for a coke, and from there on it was pattern, pure pattern. It was as easy as rolling off a girl.

He had it all figured out in a few minutes. Two dates, and a long ride in the country, and a blanket on the grass, and Sheila Kirk would be his. He was going along with the pattern, riding it out, when something snapped. He just couldn't stand it another minute. It was part of the Modnoc routine, the dulldom capital of the western world, and he wasn't going to play it that way.

He broke off in the middle of a sentence, turned to her, caught her pointed chin in one hand and looked hard into her eyes. "Look," he said to her, "how about walking over to the park and having a go at it?"

She stared. Her mouth opened, then closed again, and she went on staring some more. He felt like laughing at her.

"C'mon," he said. "We'll take a nice walk in the park and then I'll take your cruddy clothes off and it'll be good. I'm pretty great at it by now. I've been making a study of all the finer points and I'm an old pro already. What do you say to that, Sheila, old kid?"

She didn't say anything. Not a thing. She just stared.

"Come on, old girl." He took her arm and started off toward the park. She didn't seem too enthusiastic, but at the same time she walked along with him, not pulling away, not fighting a bit. It was going to be easy.

"The direct approach," he announced. "Nothing like the direct approach. You and me, Sheila, we don't have to pretend for each other. We can be honest. We can both stand a little action. We don't have to play games. We just go to the park, and lie down in the sweet-smelling grass, and we have ourselves a ball."

Which, when you come right down to it, is what they did.

He led her to a nice private place in the park, one he had used before, and there he undressed her. He didn't kiss her, mainly because he had no desire to kiss her. He took off her blouse, and he took off her bra, and he played around with two things that were closer to mountains than molehills. Then he took off the rest of her clothing, and played some more little games, and took off his own clothes, and got going.

She had been had before, and she had been had properly, and she was good at it. The shock of his approach seemed to have worn off because whatever state she was in now, it was not shock. She was squirming all over the place, and her nails were raking his back, and it was, by all rules, great.

Then they got dressed, and walked back to town, and he told her goodnight and left her to find her own way back to her house.

It was, by all rules, great. But somehow it wasn't so great at all. Somehow it was lousy, and it shouldn't have been lousy, but it was and this annoyed him. She had done a good job, and he had done a good job, and the sum total of their efforts had been highly charged monotony.

Which was a shame.

He was tired, so he went to sleep. But it took him awhile to drop off into blissful unconsciousness. He tossed around for awhile, thinking that he had to get out of Modnoc before he went out of his skull. It just wasn't fun anymore. All Modnoc ever had to offer was female flesh, and now even that was beginning to pale. It was time to go.

"I don't understand," his father said. "Don't you like it here? Don't you like living with us?"

"Frankly," Vince said, "no."

"We try to make a good home for you. We try to give you everything you want. And you just want to up and leave us. Where are you going? What are you going to do?"

Vince shrugged. "Who knows?"

"Crazy," his father said. "That's what it is, crazy. You won't finish high school and you won't go to college and you won't get a good job and—"

"Dad."

"And you'll be a bum. That's a hell of a note. I don't want a bum for a son. A thief, yes. A con man, maybe. But a bum?"

"Dad," he said. "Dad, I'm not going to be a bum."

"You're not?"

He shook his head. "I'm going to be a great success," he said. "Horatio Alger style. Spirit that made this nation the great and powerful country it is today. Young man out for success. Flash Gordon conquers the Universe. You know."

"Really?"

"Sure," Vince said, getting slightly carried away with himself. "No opportunities in a town like this. A young guy like me has a great chance in the world. Opportunities galore. Money, fame, power. All these things are waiting for a man with courage and initiative and imagination."

"You sound like an ad for door-to-door shoe salesmen."

"I'm not kidding, I'm serious, I mean it," Vince said, meaning it.

"Really?"

"Sure," Vince said. "The world is waiting for me. Maybe I'll do some traveling. Paris, Rome, Berlin. The Mysterious Orient. The South Seas. Latin America. All over the globe, challenging chances await earnest young men."

"You're not kidding," his father said, glowing.

"Nope."

"You're serious," his father said, beaming.

"Right you are."

"You mean it," his father said, bursting with pride. "My boy. My son, out for glory. A chip off the old block, that's what you are. I should have known it the minute you sold the car for six hundred dollars. You've got a head on your shoulders, Vince. A real head."

"Thanks, Dad."

"I'm proud of you, Vince. Really proud. Where are you going? Any ideas?"

"I'm not sure, Dad."

"Of course," his father said. "Of course. Got to feel your way around. Got to see which way the wind is blowing. Got to keep both feet on the ground, your nose to the grindstone, your shoulder to the wheel, all that. Hell of a position to get any work done in, but you'll manage."

"Right."

"When do you figure on leaving?"

"Well," Vince said, "I was thinking of getting started tomorrow morning."

"That's pretty soon, Vince."

"I know, but—"

"But you're one hundred percent right, boy. No time like the present. Can't let the grass grow under your feet. You know what they say about rolling stones. Don't gather any moss. But who wants moss? Right?"

"Right."

"Better let me tell your mother," Vince's father said. "You know how mothers are. Probably be all upset that her boy is leaving her.

That's the way mothers are. They sort of carry on about things like that. A tendency they have."

"Okay, Dad."

"She'll probably cry," his father said.

She did.

Vince's father didn't get enthusiastic too often, but when he did, his enthusiasm was contagious. Before she quite knew what was happening, Vince's mother agreed that Vince should go out into the cruel world. She wasn't quite sure why she thought so, but she was the type of woman who had most of her decisions made for her. She was a fine woman, a good mother and all that, but Vince's father was the real brains of the family.

Which didn't say too much for the family.

It worked out, though. Before too long, Vince had a suitcase packed and a wallet full of money. He still had most of the hundred and a half from the car, plus a little extra left over from the Saralee episode, plus the extra hundred his father pressed on him as a going-away present. When morning came, he was on his way to the bus depot. And when the bus left, he was on it.

The bus was bound for New York. That seemed like a good place to start. He had to avoid the hotel where he was known as James Blue, but in a city the size of New York that shouldn't be too hard to do. He also had to avoid Rhonda, who lived in New York, but the chances of running into her seemed pretty small. And if he did see her, he could always cross the street. It wouldn't be much trouble.

The bus moved along, the wheels churning, and Vince hummed softly to himself. The crap he had fed his father had been, strangely enough, partly true. He felt like a pioneer, a Forty-Niner heading for gold in California. Not many pioneers rode the bus, he knew, but times were changing. It was a brand-new world, a brave new world. His world.

The sun was up and the roads were clear. The bus went along at a good clip and Vince could hear the wheels singing a little song to him. He couldn't make out the words, but it was a cheerful, optimistic little song and he was happy.

Modnoc faded off into the distance. New York was ahead of him.

Chapter 9

Well, now, the best laid plans of mice and men, of mouse and man, of moose and Mau Mau, mink and marigold, as the trite and true old phrase doth say, often go astray.

Well, there was New York, and here came Vince, roaring down from the upstate foothills like a one-man tidal wave, like a time bomb ready to go off in any girl who got in his way. Well, and then here was New York and here was Vince, in the middle of Manhattan with a suitcase in his hand and a gleam in his eye. Well, and then there was New York, and where was Vince?

Vince was in Boston.

The tale of how Vince ricocheted and rebounded, how he was bank-shotted off the biggest city in the world and basketed in Boston, is one of those long sad stories without even a happy ending to make it all worthwhile. Or much of any ending at all, except that he went to Boston.

It started with the Port Authority Terminal where the bus emptied, Vince with it. He went out to the street, which was Eighth Avenue, with 41st Street to his left and 40th Street to his right. So he turned left, having had seventeen years of not going right and not wanting to change things at this late date, and a block and a half with the suitcase brought him to 42nd Street, which is the hub of half-a-dozen very strange worlds, most which Vince had no interest in.

But he had to turn right now, because the bright lights were off to the right, and there was nothing off to the left but some more street and the river, and he was too young for the river. So he turned right, in spite of himself, and lugged the suitcase toward the milling people and the flashing lights.

And a girl walked by him, crying her pretty blue eyes out.

"Hey!" That was Vince, and he said it again: "Hey!" And dropped the suitcase and started back and touched her on the arm and said it again. "Hey. What's the matter?"

"He's a bastard," the girl said, and went right on weeping. A good-looking girl she was, what the pulp-writers call class, and she was wearing a short-sleeved, full-skirted, pale blue dress of the kind that's too expensive for Saks to carry, and she had a nice young body like Spring and soft blonde hair that had been molded by the loving touch of a professional hairdresser, and even though she was weeping and strolling down 42nd Street past midnight, she had the look of lots of money, of Newport money and Palm Beach money, of private estate money and private girl's college money.

Vince took all this in while he was saying, "Who's a bastard?"

She stopped walking then, but she didn't stop weeping, and when she turned to face Vince, he saw that all that loveliness had been callously flawed by a swift right to the eye. And not too long ago either, because the swelling hadn't yet finished and the skin around the eye was only just beginning to darken. But she was going to wake up in the morning with the kind of shiner that looks cute on boys of ten but distinctly out of place on girls of twenty, particularly rich young girls who look like Spring.

"Archer is," she told him, which was the answer to his question, but he'd already forgotten all about that question and instead said, "Hey! Who hit you?"

"Archer," she said again, still crying. And started walking again.

"Hey, listen!" Vince cried. He had done a number of things in his young life, but the attempted destruction of beauty hadn't been among them, and the stirrings of a brand-new indignation was causing a flurry in his chest. "Hey, listen!" he cried. "Where is this guy? He can't do a thing like that to you!" He was trotting along after her, and glanced back once at his suitcase, sitting in the middle of the empty sidewalk, then trotted on because suitcases always come second after beauty.

"He's a bastard," she said again, and the word seemed as out-of-place on her lips as the shiner did on her eye.

"Listen!" Vince cried, caught up in the romance of the thing. "Tell me where he is! Tell me where he is, and I'll take care of him for you!"

She stopped and turned to him with a glad cry. "Would you?"

Vince had never before felt like a knight-errant, but there's a first time for everything. "Damn right I will!" he cried, and shook his fist.

The girl had stopped weeping to beam at him, and now she stopped beaming to frown and look doubtful. "But why would you?" she wanted to know. "You don't even know me."

Vince tried to put it into words, and it wasn't all that easy. "A girl like you," he started. "A girl as good-looking as you—to punch a girl in the eye—" He stopped, took a deep breath, and shouted, "He can't do a thing like that, that's all!"

"Do you really mean it?" she demanded.

"Of course I mean it!"

"He's gone home," she said. She reached out and touched his arm and she must have been carrying a load of static electricity because the touch of her fingers on his arm jolted him to his soul. "He's gone back to his apartment," she went on. "I'll take you there."

"I'll show him!" cried Vince.

"My car is down here," said the girl. "In the parking lot."

He went with her three steps, then stopped. "My suitcase," he said. "Wait, I'll only be a minute." She waited, and he ran back, to discover that an agitator with a Bible had taken up a stance on the sidewalk next to his bag, and a crowd had gathered around to punctuate his appeal with good-natured obscenities, and it took Vince a couple minutes to worm his way through the Philistines to the suitcase and back. "Are you saved?" cried the agitator, and Vince shouted, "I'm going to be!" and ran back to the girl who looked like Spring.

She led him to the parking lot and to her car, which not surprisingly turned out to be a Mercedes-Benz 190 SL which, while not the hottest car on the road today, is the hottest one that isn't actually on fire.

They got in the car and she drove. She wasn't crying anymore, but looking furious and determined, and as they snaked through the cabs she told him one or two things. "His name is Archer Danile," she said. And a minute later: "I'm Anita Merriweather."

"Vince," he told her.

She nodded and was silent and sneaked between a cab and a truck and shot through a red light and made a right turn without taking her foot off the accelerator. "We were out tonight," she said all at once. "And we got into an argument. He was drunk, and he hit me."

"The bastard!" Vince cried. The girl's wild driving didn't scare him, it exhilarated him. This was all he'd been missing in Modnoc. Action and adventure and romance, and the feeling of adrenalin coursing through him and his pulse pounding and he was, by God, a bloody knight errant.

She drove and drove and then stopped, and they were on East 63rd Street between Madison and Park Avenue, which is what you call a ritzy address. They got out of the car and went into a building, and they were in a square little place that was mainly marble. The street doors were behind them, another set of doors was ahead of them, and the square metal bank of mailboxes and doorbells was to their right.

"When he asks who it is," she said, "I'll answer. He'll let me in. Then we can go up and you can take care of him."

"Right," Vince said. He clenched his fists and hunched his shoulders and knew he could lick the world.

The girl—Anita—pressed a button and a minute later a blurry voice said, "Who's there?" and she leaned close to the mouthpiece to answer, "Anita." And a buzzing sound came immediately from the door.

They went in and there was a wide long room like a hall, with a mirror and a table and a vase full of flowers and a self-service elevator. They zoomed up to the eleventh floor and down the hall, and Vince waited beside the door, out of sight of the peephole, while Anita rang the bell.

Click went the peephole, and click again, and then the door opened, and Anita walked in. Vince followed.

The door led to a hall, which went away to the left, to the living room. Anita walked down the hall and Vince followed, and there didn't seem to be anyone else in the apartment at all, which was ridiculous.

Anita turned around to frown in puzzlement at Vince, and her eyes widened and she cried, "Behind you!"

Vince turned. This Archer Danile had been behind the door, which was now closed, and he was coming grinning down the hall toward Vince. He was tall and blond and Greek-goddish, which is to say somewhere between Apollo and Bacchus. And Vince looked at him and knew he had better smite the first blow, because there might not be a second.

So he stepped forward to the grinning Greek god and punched him square in the nose. And Archer Danile went, "Uck!" and half-turned, and leaned against the wall. His profile was plain before Vince's eyes, all manly nose and manly jaw, and Vince snapped another fist out, lacing across the manly jaw, and Danile went "Urk!" again, and fell down.

"Hit him!" cried Anita. "Hit him!" More strange words to come from the mouth of a girl who looked like Spring.

"Quite enough," Danile said clumsily. He was sitting on the floor, looking at the opposite wall, and trying quite unsuccessfully to smile. "Quite enough," he repeated, just as clumsily. "You've already broken my jaw."

"Your jaw?" Vince had been standing there, fists clenched, waiting for Danile to get up and rejoin the fray. Now he eased the taut fingers and leaned forward to look at Danile's face. It did seem different now, he noticed, a trifle unbalanced. The jaw seemed to be a bit too far to the left.

"You've done it this time, Anita," said Danile, still trying to smile and still looking across at the opposite wall. "You've really done it this time."

"Well, look what you did to me!" The girl pushed past Vince and leaned forward, pointing at her eye.

Vince all at once felt left out. The two were comparing wounds, and Vince didn't have any interesting malfunctions worth mentioning. Not only that, but the romance and high adventure were quite rapidly leaving this whole episode. The whole thing was suddenly a disappointment. For one thing, it hadn't actually been a fight he'd had with Archer Danile. He'd punched the man twice, knocked him down, and broken his jaw. And he didn't even *know* him!

For another thing, he didn't even know Anita Merriweather. He'd been walking along, minding his own business—

She was tugging him by the elbow. "Come on," she was saying. "We've got to get out of here."

"You've done it this time, Anita," said Archer Danile mildly.

Vince allowed her to lead him from the apartment and down the hall to the elevator and down the elevator to the first floor and out the door and into the Mercedes-Benz 190 SL.

"You'll have to come home with me," said Anita.

"Okay," said Vince. He had given up thought for the duration and was simply letting things happen.

Anita jumped on the accelerator as though it were Archer Danile's head, and they shot away from the curb and down the street.

After one or two blocks, Vince's mind began once more to work. And, Vince's mind being what it was, the first thing he thought of was sex.

Sex with Anita Merriweather, that was. If anything was obvious in this green world, it was that Anita Merriweather wasn't part of the greenery. That is, she wasn't green. To put it simply, she was unvirginal. It was plain, that is, that she was not a virgin.

Because, of course, she'd been living with that guy. Right? Of course. There wasn't any question. And besides, she was rich, and everyone knew what the rich did. Even more often than the poor. And with more people. And started younger.

And besides that, she had invited him to her place. Which meant only one thing. He had beaten up her old boyfriend for her, and he was on his way to get his reward. And his reward would be—Anita.

There had been a time when such a reward would have filled Vince with mouth-watering anticipation. But that time had ended somewhere in the last month, and now, instead, he wondered where the romance and adventure had gone, and he wondered further if it wouldn't be a good idea to just step out of this hot little car the next time Anita decided to obey a traffic light, and wander off into the city again.

But it was nearly one o'clock in the morning, and Anita was offering, besides her body, a place to sleep. That would be nice. And in the morning he could begin again and afresh, and henceforward he would ignore all weeping girls, even weeping girls who look like Spring and dress like money.

Anita was silent now, and so was Vince, and they drove and they drove. They crossed a bridge, and that startled him at first, until he realized that a girl like this, wealthy and all, undoubtedly would live on Long Island. So he relaxed and lit a cigarette, and they drove and drove.

And they kept on driving, they just kept on diving, and Vince noticed that they were on a major highway.

"Hey! Where do you live, anyway?" he asked.

"Boston," she said, and kept on driving.

So that was how Vince happened to go to Boston. He hadn't planned on going to Boston, he hadn't even ever thought much about Boston, one way or the other. But there he was, at six o'clock in the morning, in Boston. They drove around the Common, and up Beacon Hill, and then they stopped, and they were parked in a driveway beside a mansion.

"Come in," said Anita, and she got out of the car and walked away, toward the back of the mansion.

Vince scrabbled for his suitcase, and once more he trotted after the girl, and they went in a back door and down three steps and they were in a kitchen. A huge kitchen, with three white walls and the fourth wall of unpainted brick. There was a big wooden table and wooden chairs and a strange combination of the most modern (refrigerator and freezer and dishwasher) with the most antique (a wood-burning stove and shelves lined with intricately designed china).

"Sit down," Anita said, and Vince sat down.

"I bet you could use some coffee," Anita said, and Vince nodded.

He was stunned and he was exhausted. It had been quite a while since he'd slept, and so everything that happened in the world outside his eyes happened in a strange slow-motion sort of way, and he had plenty of leisure to be stunned about things that were surprising.

And Anita was surprising. And Boston was surprising. And his presence in this kitchen was surprising. So he just sat there and waited for whatever was going to happen next.

And he knew something was going to happen next. He'd been feeling strange ever since he'd first noticed Anita, weeping and black-eyed, go walking by him, back on 42nd Street in New York. And now, like Anita's shiner, that strange feeling within him had grown and grown, and he knew that something fantastic was going to happen, and he didn't know what it was, and he didn't even know if it were going to be good or bad.

She had a hell of a shiner by now, a swollen black discoloration around the left eye, but instead of marring her, it merely emphasized the beauty of the rest of her. A beautiful girl, who moved like a racehorse and looked like a debutante's self-delusion, and who was going to be a prime mover in the strange happenstance that Vince could feel coming upon him.

She sat down with him at the table, bringing with her two steaming mugs of black coffee, and she said, "Tell me about yourself."

"You first," he countered, not knowing why, but only knowing that that was the thing to say.

"All right," she said. She smiled and shrugged, and said, "I'm Anita Merriweather. My parents have lots of money. I'm twenty years old and I don't know what I want, but it isn't anything I have. I hate Archer Danile and everybody like him, parasites, drifters. That's what the argument was about. I went to college two years and then I stopped, because there wasn't anything there I wanted. I've been to Europe and I've been to Japan, and I don't feel as though I've been anywhere. I'm young and I *feel* young, and I want to grow up. And now it's your turn."

"I'm Vince," he said. And then he told her about himself, and he told her the truth. He told her about his summer, about his virgin hunt and about Saralee and about pimping and leaving the car and telling his father he was going out into the big wide world to seek his fortune. She laughed at the right places, and she looked serious at the right places, and when he was finished she said, "I wish I'd been with you. I wish I'd been along for every minute of that. I don't know anything. I've never had anything except money, and that isn't enough."

He looked at her, and he felt the happening coming on, getting ready to burst, and he opened his mouth to give it a chance to happen, and when his mouth was open he said, "Will you marry me?" And he hadn't known that was what was going to happen.

And she smiled at him. And she said, "Yes."

"Anita," he said. It was all he could say. He didn't even know her, and a million pieces of common sense were clamoring for his attention, were hollering at him that he couldn't propose marriage to a girl he'd met six hours ago, and he ignored them all.

"Vince," she said, and looked at him, and her one good eye was as deep as a bottomless abyss, and he knew he was teetering on the edge of that bottomless abyss, and he knew he was going to topple in.

He got to his feet. "Come on," he said.

"Yes," she said.

She had to lead the way, because it was her house and not his and he didn't know where her room was. They left the kitchen and they walked through one room after another, and through halls and corridors, and up a flight of stairs, and around them all the way was the kind of richness Vince had only seen in old movies on television.

And finally they came to a closed door and Anita opened it and they went in and she closed the door behind them. It was a big room, as big as the whole cottage had been back at the miserable lake, and across on the other side of the room were three windows, with the early morning sunshine pouring in. And midway between the door and the windows, its headboard against the right-hand wall, was a bed, Anita's bed.

She turned to him to say, "You haven't even kissed me yet." And her voice broke when she said it, and he knew that she was as terrified as he.

He reached for her, and she came slim-waisted and eager into his arms, and he kissed her. And her lips were soft and cool-warm, and her tongue was a slender reed playing with his thick bear of a tongue, and her body was slender and like Spring against him.

He kissed her, and then she moved away, crossing the room, making a wide berth around the bed, going to the window, looking out and down, her face and hair highlighted by the sun, and she was the slimmest, youngest, most beautiful, most heart-wrenchingly perfect thing he had ever seen in all his life.

Betty and Rhonda and Adele and Saralee and all the others ceased to exist. He could feel them receding away from him, like smoke, evaporating, and he felt a momentary sadness at their departure, and then he didn't care anymore, because the blonde-haired girl dressed in blue, made up for all of them, and was all he would ever need.

He came across the room to her, feeling himself lumbering and clumsy, wishing he were lighter, more graceful, more accomplished, more an ideal, to match the ideal that she was. He came across the room, and he touched her arm, as he had done years ago in New York on 42nd Street near Eighth Avenue, and he said, "I love you, Anita."

"I love you, Vince," she said.

It was a ritual, like the marriage ceremony, except that it was much more solemn and much more binding. And he held her arm and turned her around and kissed her again. And their clothes seemed to float away, like gossamer and lace in the barest of breezes. They were naked, and hand in hand they walked to the wide sunlit bed.

Her body was Spring, was young and Spring.

She was closed to him at first, and her clear brow ruffled in a frown as her lips whispered, "Vince." And then she sighed, and her good eye closed, and his lips were by her cheek, and he murmured her name, "Anita. Anita. Anita."

And they flowed together, blended together, and the sweatiness of the past disappeared, and he understood now why he had lost interest in all those others. It was because he had needed this completion, this unhurried blending, this oneness.

•   •   •

"You were a virgin!"

"Yes," she said.

The sound of the door opening spun him around on the bed.

A woman, fiftyish, tall and prim, obviously Anita's mother, stood wide-eyed on the threshold. Her eyebrows lifted and she looked at Vince. "I don't believe I know you," she said.

Chapter 10

"All I have to say," Anita was saying, "is that Baltimore is an unusual place for a honeymoon."

"What's wrong with Baltimore?"

"Nothing," Anita said, "is wrong with Baltimore. Nothing could possibly be wrong with Baltimore. Don't misunderstand me. I like Baltimore. I love Baltimore. I—"

"How about the Lord Baltimore Hotel?"

"A wonderful hotel," Anita said. "A magnificent hotel. The food in the Oak Room is delicious. The decor in the lobby is exquisite. The service is impeccable. The furniture is posh and the rugs are thick. The view breathtaking. The—"

"How about the room?"

"The room," said Anita, "is sumptuous. It has a television set with a thirty-inch screen. You don't even have to drop in a quarter to make it operate. And—"

"How about the bed?"

"Mmmmmmmmm," said Anita.

"You like the bed?"

"I love the bed."

"Well," said Vince, "we're on it."

"True."

"And, after all, it's our honeymoon."

"True."

"Sooooo—"

"A good idea," said Anita. "An excellent idea. A commendable idea. But do you think we ought to again?"

"It's our wedding night," Vince reminded her. "Wedding nights only come once a marriage."

"Well," said Anita, running her hands over him, "I wouldn't want to put up a fight. But you have to be gentle. After all, I used to be a virgin. You have to bear that in mind."

"Yes, Santa Claus," Vince murmured. "There was a virgin."

The chain of circumstances that got Vince and Anita from a bed in Boston to a bed in Baltimore is a curious chain of circumstances indeed. When we last saw Vince, as you may recall, he was under the watchful eyes of Mrs. Merriweather, who happened to be Anita's mother. Anita's mother, strange to say, was not too pleased with the spectacle of Vince and her daughter lying belly-to-belly. She was, as a matter of fact, somewhat livid with rage.

"I'll have you thrown in jail," she ranted. "I carry a lot of weight in this country, young man. I'll have your father thrown off the stock exchange. I'll ruin your entire family. I'll—"

"Mother," said Anita gently, "shut up."

Mrs. Merriweather shut up.

"In the first place," Anita said, "we haven't all been properly introduced. Vince, this is Helen Merriweather, my mother. Mother, this is Vince. Uh . . . I don't know your last name—"

Vince supplied his last name.

"That," said Anita, "is the first place. In the second place, you are not going to have anybody thrown into jail. Vince has done nothing wrong. If anybody is going to land in jail, it will be me."

"You?" said Vince and Mrs. Merriweather in one voice.

"Me. I am twenty years old and Vince is only seventeen. This makes me guilty of statutory rape, mother. You wouldn't want to see your daughter in jail, would you?"

Mrs. Merriweather shuddered.

"That," said Anita, "takes care of two places. In the third and final place, Vince and I are going to be married."

"Married?" said Mrs. Merriweather.

"Married," said Vince and Anita in one voice.

"What you just had the unmitigated gall to intrude upon the aftermath of," said Anita, "is what is technically referred to as premarital intercourse. While you and Beacon Hill may feel that it is not proper form, it has happened. Once. Tonight. Tomorrow we will be married, and tonight's escapade will be justified ex post facto. I feel certain you can see the value of that."

"Anita," Mrs. Merriweather said, "you must remember that you are not old enough to marry without my consent. I have some voice in this matter."

"True," said Anita. "But you will give your consent."

"I will?"

"Of course," said Anita. "Otherwise Vince and I will live in sin on the front lawn. Just think how the neighbors would react to *that*."

Mrs. Merriweather thought how the neighbors would react to *that*. "You wouldn't do it," she said levelly. "You wouldn't."

Anita said nothing.

"You wouldn't," Mrs. Merriweather repeated weakly. "Would you?"

"Yes," said Anita. "I would."

"You probably would," Mrs. Merriweather agreed. "Knowing you, you probably would. I wouldn't put it past you."

Mrs. Merriweather smiled. It was, Vince thought, a strange smile. Any smile under such circumstances had to be a strange smile. Perhaps, Vince guessed, the hallmark of the wealthy was their ability to smile when there was nothing to smile about. At any rate, Mrs. Merriweather seemed determined to make the best of a bad thing. Vince was the bad thing.

"Well," said Mrs. Merriweather, "I shall give my consent. Not gleefully, I admit. But stoically. However, I don't see how you can arrange to be married tomorrow. There's a waiting period, you know. Two or three days."

"We can't wait that long," Anita said.

And Vince, who had felt for a few minutes as though they were going to have the wedding without him because he was so thoroughly excluded from the conversation, chimed in with a valuable thought. "There's no waiting period in Maryland," he said. "We can fly down to Baltimore and be married immediately."

"Baltimore," said Anita thoughtfully.

"Baltimore," said Mrs. Merriweather, heavily.

"Baltimore," said Vince, happily.

"Baltimore," said Anita, decisively. "Now, mother, if you'll leave us alone, Vince and I would like to get some sleep."

"Together?"

"Together," Vince and Anita said, together.

"But—"

"Of course," said Anita, "there's always the front lawn—"

Mrs. Merriweather sighed. Then, with the air of someone making the best of a bad thing, she suggested: "Vince, Anita, before you go to sleep again, there's one thing I'd like to do for you."

"What is it?"

"You may object," Mrs. Merriweather said. "Old practical people sometimes have old practical ideas which conflict with the notions of romantic youth. But still—"

"Get to the point, Mother."

"If you don't mind," Mrs. Merriweather said timorously, "I'd rather like to change that sheet."

There was, inevitably, a two-day waiting period in Baltimore. There had to be a two-day waiting period in Baltimore, of course. The wedding would not have been complete without it. The two of them, Anita and Vince, taxied at breathtaking speed from the Baltimore airport to City Hall, raced hysterically down the corridor to the License Bureau, and were informed that there was a two-day waiting period in the state of Maryland. Anita threw a fit, and then they laughed, and then they prepared to spend two days in Baltimore waiting for it to be time to get married.

Which is to say that they had their honeymoon before the wedding.

"It's not really that bad," Vince explained. "After all, we don't really know each other. This way we have a chance to know each other. By the time the two days are up, we will be prepared for marriage. It's a lucky break, this waiting period."

"Sure," Anita said. "Except I'm in a rush to be married. I hate this waiting."

"You hate *this*?"

"Not that."

"And *this*?"

"Well, not that."

"How about . . . *this*?"

"Vince—"

"Well, do you?"

"Vince," she whispered throatily. "Vince, you shouldn't do that. It gets me all excited. It gets me so excited I can't stand it. It makes me want you to make love to me."

"Good," Vince said. "I was beginning to think along those lines myself."

They were married, finally, after two heavenly but interminable days had come and gone. They were married in a minister's study, with Vince wearing a once-pressed suit and with Anita wearing a black dress. It was, all things considered, a somewhat bizarre ceremony. Vince was shaking throughout it, wondering what, in addition to Anita, he was getting into. But it went more or less according to plan, and then they were married, and away they went, back to the hotel and to bed.

And to bed. And to bed. And to bed. And to bed.

The night lasted a long time. So, for that matter, did the morning. Then, suddenly, it was noon, and time to leave the hotel, and face the world. They showered, dressed, packed, and left.

"We have to see my parents," Vince said, remembering that he had some and that they had something of a right to know of his new station in life. "They live in Modnoc. I think I told you about them."

"You did."

"We have to see them," Vince repeated. "Tell them we're married. Get their blessing. That sort of thing."

"They won't like me," Anita said.

"Of course they will. They'll love you. You're young and sweet and beautiful."

"I'm older than you."

"So what?"

"They'll think I'm an old lady corrupting an innocent youth. Actually, of course, it's the other way around. You corrupted me. Nobody on earth could corrupt you. You're as corrupt as can be."

"And," Vince reminded her, "you like it that way."

"Love it," said Anita. "But your parents will hate me."

They didn't. Vince cleverly managed to see his father first. He and Anita walked into the office while his father was working. And his father was his usual self.

"Vince," he said. "Vince. My boy. You're back already. Good to see you, Vince. Did you take the world by storm? Carve your name on the face of the nation? Eh, boy? What stories of success have you brought back to your old Dad?"

"Dad," Vince said, "this is Anita."

Eyes glanced briefly at Anita, took her in. Teeth flashed briefly in a smile. Then the eyes flashed back to Vince. "That's nice," he said. "Nice girl. Always glad to meet one of your girlfriends, Vince. But let's get back to you. How have you been doing, my boy? Making your way in the world? Getting ahead by bounds and leaps? Setting the world on fire?"

"Well," said Vince.

"If it's money," Vince's father said, "I understand. I'll be glad to help out. World's a tough place. How much do you need?"

"Dad," Vince said, "Anita isn't a girlfriend."

Vince's father looked a little stunned. He had more or less forgotten Anita, and now the conversation was back to her for some incomprehensible reason, and his son was telling him that she wasn't a girlfriend. "Then what is she?"

"My wife," Vince said.

"Your *what*?"

"My wife," Vince said firmly.

"Your WHAT?"

Anita put a small tentative hand on the shaking shoulder of Vince's father. "Steady," she said. "You mustn't let yourself get upset. Bad for the heart."

Vince's father relaxed. Somewhat.

"Vince and I were married," Anita was saying now. "Two days ago in Baltimore. We fell in love and decided to get married. Now we are man and wife. For better or for worse. That sort of thing."

"For worse," Vince's father said. "Obviously, for worse. Vince is only seventeen. You can't get married at seventeen. It doesn't make any sense."

"We're in love," Vince said.

"Then sleep together," his father suggested, taking a totally opposite stand from that of Anita's mother. "Sleep together. On the front lawn, if you want. But don't get married. For God's sake, don't get married."

"We already did," Anita said.

"In Baltimore," Vince added.

"WHY?"

"Because we're in love," Anita said.

"Deeply in love," Vince added.

"Oh," said Vince's father. Then: "But how in the name of heaven do you expect to keep body and soul together? You don't know what it costs to support a wife, Vince. Takes a lot of money. And you were going to be a success, remember? Horatio Alger? That sort of thing? There's an old saying, my boy. He who takes on wife and children gives hostages to fame and fortune."

"Children?" Anita said. "Not for a while, I hope."

"You never know," Vince's father said darkly. "They have a way of coming up when you least expect them." And he looked at Vince with a reminiscent gleam in his eye.

"But," he said suddenly, "let's get back to money. Maybe it'll work if you're planning on having Anita get a job. Maybe the two of you can get to work together. Can you type, Anita? Take shorthand? Keep books?"

"I can't do anything," Anita said.

"Oh," Vince's father said. "Well, where there's a will, there's a way. Old saying. You can learn. You're young. You—"

Vince felt called upon to explain. His father didn't understand the basic nature of the situation. He had to fill his old man in. He meant well, his father did, but he was missing a few salient points.

"Dad," he said slowly, "money is no problem."

"Ah," his father said, "it never is when you're seventeen. But it becomes more of a problem as you grow older. You probably think you can live on love. All the old myths. Two can live as cheaply as one. Not true, young lovers. Two can live as cheaply as one if only one eats. Otherwise it doesn't work out that way.

Has a way of surprising you. Oh, I know I sound like a materialistic old fool. But money matters, Vince. Money makes a big difference. Why, I remember when your mother and I got married. Didn't have a pot to cook in, as the old expression goes. We thought it would be easy. But—"

"Dad," Vince broke in desperately, "Anita's father has better than five million dollars."

For perhaps the first time in his life, Vince's father was at a loss for words. He stood there with his mouth hanging open. He looked as though someone had hit him over the head with a bankbook.

"Five million dollars," Vince repeated reverently. "So money is no problem. Not for us. I mean—"

"Excuse me," Vince's father said, recovering slightly. He looked at Anita. "What did you say your name was?"

"It was Anita Merriweather. Now it's—"

"I know what it is now," Vince's father said. "Merriweather. Not the iron-and-steel Merriweathers?"

"That's my uncle," Anita said. "Dad is the brokerage Merriweathers."

Vince's father sat down. Heavily. "Five million dollars," he said softly. "Five million dollars. Vince, my boy, I don't know how you do it. You know, I had my doubts when you set out to conquer the world. Didn't want to voice them, but I'll admit now that I had my doubts. Couldn't figure out how you'd make a lot of money. Oh, I know you've got the brains for it. No question about that. But the way the tax set-up goes these days, I didn't think you could come out ahead of the game. Hell, a man can't get rich by earning money these days. But you found the answer, you genius.

You did it, you hero. There's only one way to get money, and that's to marry it, and that's just what you did."

"Not for money," Vince said.

"For love," Anita explained.

"We're in love," Vince said.

"Deeply in love," Anita said.

"Forever and ever," Vince said.

"Amen," Vince's father said. "Amen and amen. Well, I guess money's no problem, after all. How about that?"

Vince and Anita smiled.

"Vince," his father said, "your mother doesn't know yet, does she? I mean, you haven't told her about the wedding, have you?"

"Not yet. We wanted to tell you first."

"Good idea. Fine idea. Well, I think you ought to let me break it to her. Sort of let her in on it a little at a time. You know how mothers are. But I'm sure she'll like Anita. Of course she will. Wonderful girl, Anita."

Vince and Anita beamed.

"She'll probably cry," Vince's father said thoughtfully.

She did.

But tears have a way of stopping. Vince's mother, being a woman all the way, was considerably less impressed by five million dollars than was Vince's father. She thought the money was nice, of course, and of course she wasn't going to hold it against Anita, but that wasn't the turning point. Neither, as it happened, was Vince's father's firm assurance that they had not lost a son but had gained a daughter. This turned out to be about as reassuring as it was original. The big thing was not what was said but Anita herself.

Vince's mother talked to Anita, and Vince's mother looked at Anita, and before long Vince's mother decided that Anita happened to be just what Vince needed. Since Vince and Anita had already agreed on this point, there was no conflict there. Before long Vince's mother was writing out little file cards with Vince's favorite recipes on them, and otherwise preparing Anita for what was obviously the most important role in life, that of Vince's wife. Anita cared about as much for cooking as she cared for crocheting lace doilies, but she wisely kept quiet. Everybody approved of everybody. The parents thought Anita was a darling girl, and Anita thought the parents were darling parents, and life was suddenly very much worth living.

They stayed in Modnoc for two weeks. They stayed in Vince's room, and that made Vince understand that they were very definitely married and that it was very definitely right for them to be married. He had slept with many women in his young life, but this was the first time he had ever slept with a woman in his own room in his own house. He thought it would feel wrong, but it didn't, and when things really got going he barely knew where he was, so everything was all right.

And then, at last, it was time to leave Modnoc. It was time to go back to Boston, to meet Anita's father, who somehow had been left out of the picture. Vince wasn't especially looking forward to the meeting. From one standpoint, Mr. Merriweather was the great benefactor, the man with the five million dollars, the great white father who would see to it that Vince never had to work for the rest of his life. That was one way of looking at it, but it was not necessarily the right way.

The other side of the coin had Mr. Merriweather playing the role of indignant papa, prepared to disown his willful daughter and to cast his new son-in-law out into the street, penniless. This was a far less attractive picture. From what Anita had said of her father, old man Merriweather was a twentieth-century improvement on the concept of the self-made man. He hadn't exactly dragged himself up out of the gutter. But he had taken the three hundred thousand dollars his father had left him and turned it into five million. Which, all things considered, was no mean accomplishment. Even if you're born with a silver spoon in your mouth, it's a neat trick turning it into a platinum one.

And what self-made man was going to look with favor upon a penniless son-in-law with the hand out? Not Mr. Merriweather. Not in a million years.

Actually, Vince didn't find either prospect particularly attractive. He wasn't too keen on being disinherited, for obvious reasons. But at the same time he wasn't too hot on the notion of living off Papa for the rest of his life. Somehow that took the kicks out of the game. It was sort of like settling down in Modnoc, except without a job. The same monotony, on a solid gold Cadillac level. The same lack of incentive and stimulation. It would be easier to bear, due to the presence of the most wonderful girl in the world, but he couldn't help wondering how long it would take for even that to wear thin. If he didn't work, and if everything got handed to him on a platinum platter, then he and Anita were going to have a rough time of it.

"Don't you worry about a thing," Anita would say. "Papa will be perfectly wonderful about the whole thing. There's an answer, somewhere in the middle, maybe. We'll find it."

Vince pretended to be very optimistic about the whole thing, but he remained scared. And the scared feeling did not vanish when he met Mr. Merriweather. It grew.

Mr. Merriweather wasn't the type of man with whom you felt instantly relaxed. He was the type of man who made you feel as though your tie was crooked. Even if you didn't happen to be wearing a tie. He was big, and he was white-haired, and he stood at attention even when he was sitting down. He smelled of money and hard work simultaneously and Vince felt intimidated.

"Always figured Anita would do something like this," he said. "Type of girl she is. High-spirited. Red-blooded. Sets her head and heart on something and doesn't let go. Can't fight her, whether I approve or not. Don't know whether I approve or not. You good for anything, Vince? You got any ambitions? Any ideas? Or are you going to sponge off the old man and wait for him to die?"

Vince was struck dumb. He hoped he didn't look stupid but was sure that he did. He felt stupid. That much was certain.

"Maybe you don't want to be a playboy," Mr. Merriweather said. "Maybe you want me to get you started in my business. Slip you into a junior executive slot at, say, twenty thousand a year. Move you up quickly, make a branch manager out of you or something. Wouldn't have to do much of anything. Take a vacation whenever you felt like it, put in a couple hours a day at a desk the rest of the time. Give you a good position with enough money and enough respectability. That what you're angling for?"

"No," said a voice. Vince looked around. Then he realized that it was his voice.

"No?"

"No," Vince said, more positively this time. "I don't want any favors. Whatever I get I'm going to work for. It's not my fault if your daughter happened to be blessed with a rich father. I didn't have anything to do with that. Neither did she. Whatever Anita and I have, we're going to have for ourselves. And we're going to get it by ourselves. Without any handouts."

Mr. Merriweather's eyebrows went up. "You're a good actor," he said. "You almost make me believe that you're sincere."

"Almost?"

"Almost," Anita's father said. "But not entirely. Nobody throws money away. Self-respect is all well and good, but nobody turns down the sort of opportunity I just offered you. I'm afraid I don't believe you, son."

Vince bristled. "That's just too goddamned bad," he said. "Because I don't happen to give a damn whether you believe me or not. You can take your job and stick it up your—"

"Vince!" Merriweather's eyes blazed. "No one talks to me like that."

"I do," Vince said.

"Maybe more people should," Merriweather said. "You know, I do believe you now. It's ridiculous, of course, but I believe you. You're a fool, of course, but maybe the world needs more fools."

Vince, naturally, kept his fat mouth shut. He was wondering why he hadn't kept his fat mouth shut before, when he had an offer of twenty thousand dollars a year for doing nothing. Now he had no offer at all, which was substantially less.

"Vince," Mr. Merriweather was saying, "perhaps I have something else you might be interested in. Not as attractive, but something."

"I don't want a handout, Mr. Merriweather."

"This isn't a handout. Are you interested?"

"Maybe."

Merriweather laughed. It was quite a laugh. He threw back his head and broke the room in half with his laughter. "You little wise guy," he said. "You sharpie. How old are you, Vince?"

"Seventeen."

"Just seventeen? You certainly aren't the normal seventeen-year-old. What made you grow up so fast? Good Lord, the average youngster these days is a perfect example of stunted development. Four years of high school, four years of college, four years of graduate study—and the result is less mature than you are. Can you explain that? Was there any particular factor that made you grow up?"

Someone—it couldn't possibly have been Vince—said: "Women."

Merriweather's laugh made the other laugh sound like a chuckle. "That's it!" he said. "That's the trouble with modern man. No rakes left in the world. A batch of sincere idiots. You must have been a real lady killer, Vince."

Vince lowered his head modestly.

"That's the secret," Merriweather said. "Love 'em and leave 'em before you marry. Then stick to one woman. That's the way I did it. I must have had . . . oh, I don't know, but there were a hell of a lot of them. Then I met Helen and that was it for me. Strict fidelity. Uh . . . you will be faithful to Anita, won't you?"

"Of course," Vince said. "When you've had the best—"

"Precisely," Mr. Merriweather said. "Vince, if someone had said you would turn out to be a boy after my own heart, I would have laughed in his face. But you're all right, Vince. You're too young for the offer I have in mind, but I think you might be able to handle it. Know what I'm getting at?"

"No."

"Simple," Merriweather said. "Our house is thinking of opening a Brazilian branch; dealing primarily in Brazilian securities. There's a fortune to be made down there. They're short of capital. The right investments will move at triple the speed of comparable investments Stateside. A Brazilian realty syndicate will pay thirty percent compared to an American ten percent. Brazilian stocks either fall flat or double every two months. It's the perfect spot for a brokerage office. A smart man down there can get rich overnight. Or go completely broke. It's up to the man involved."

Vince wisely didn't say anything.

"Interested?"

"In what?"

Merriweather smiled. "You'll spend three months in the New York office," he said. "You'll make fifty dollars a week and you'll hustle your behind off for it. Then you go down to Brazil—if you can stand the gaff. You'll be second-in-command of the Sao Paolo office. You'll put in twenty hours a day for a relatively small salary. But if you play your cards right, you'll come out of there with a fortune in your pocket. It's all up to you, Vince. If you make money, it's your own money. If you lose, I won't be around to bail you out. It's all up to you."

"I'll take it," Vince said.

"It's not soft," Merriweather said. "It's hard. I don't know if I would take it myself, come to think of it. I don't know if I'd have the guts."

"I think you would," Vince said.

Merriweather studied him. "I think you'll wind up broke," he said. "I think you'll come out of Brazil with your hat in your hand, begging me for a soft touch."

"Don't bet on it," Vince said.

It was the middle of January and the sun was hotter than hell. The summer in Brazil came in the middle of winter. And when it was hot, hell was no hotter.

"I picked a winner," Anita said. "I picked a real winner. You keep surprising me, Vince. And you keep winning."

"Write your father," Vince said. "Let him know about it."

"He knows."

"It looks as though the Moreno Dam is going through," Vince said. "We've got a piece of it."

"Good," Anita said.

"We're doing all right," Vince said. "We're doing fine. By the way, I love you."

"You do?"

"Uh-huh. Quit hogging the pillow."

"Sorry."

"Comfortable bed," Vince said. "Comfortable girl. You busy, little girl?"

"It's awfully hot."

"It can get hotter."

"In this heat?"

"I'm strong," Vince said. "And young. Come here, little one."

The bed creaked and the world sang.

My Newsletter: I get out an email newsletter at unpredictable intervals, but rarely more often than every other week. I'll be happy to add you to the distribution list. A blank email to lawbloc@gmail.com with "newsletter" in the subject line will get you on the list, and a click of the "Unsubscribe" link will get you off it, should you ultimately decide you're happier without it.

Lawrence Block has been writing award-winning mystery and suspense fiction for half a century. You can read his thoughts about crime fiction and crime writers in *The Crime of Our Lives*, where this MWA Grand Master tells it straight. His most recent novels are *The Girl With the Deep Blue Eyes*; *The Burglar Who Counted the Spoons*, featuring Bernie Rhodenbarr; *Hit Me,* featuring Keller; and *A Drop of the Hard Stuff,* featuring Matthew Scudder, played by Liam Neeson in the film *A Walk Among the Tombstones.* Several of his other books have been filmed, although not terribly well. He's well known for his books for writers, including the classic *Telling Lies for Fun &f Profit,* and *The Liar's Bible.* In addition to prose works, he has written episodic television (*Tilt!*) and the Wong Kar-wai film, *My Blueberry Nights.* He is a modest and humble fellow, although you would never guess as much from this biographical note.

Email: lawbloc@gmail.com
Twitter: @LawrenceBlock
Facebook: lawrence.block
Website: lawrenceblock.com

CPSIA information can be obtained
at www.ICGtesting.com
Printed in the USA
LVHW010329100821
694914LV00011B/1551